Library of Congress Cataloging-in-Publication Data

Names: Bearce, Stephanie, author.
Title: Twisted true tales from science : insane inventors / by Stephanie
  Bearce.
Other titles: Insane inventors
Description: Waco, Texas : Prufrock Press, Inc., [2017] | Audience: Ages
  9-12. | Includes bibliographical references.
Identifiers: LCCN 2016051031 | ISBN 9781618215703 (pbk.)
Subjects: LCSH: Inventors--Biography--Juvenile literature. |
  Inventions--History--Juvenile literature.
Classification: LCC T39 .B43 2017 | DDC 609.22--dc23
LC record available at https://lccn.loc.gov/2016051031

Edited by Lacy Compton

Cover and layout design by Raquel Trevino
Illustrations by Eliza Bolli

ISBN-13: 978-1-61821-570-3

Printed in the United States of America.

At the time of this book's publication, all facts and figures cited are the most current available. All telephone numbers, addresses, and website URLs are accurate and active. All publications, organizations, websites, and other resources exist as described in the book, and all have been verified. The author and Prufrock Press Inc. make no warranty or guarantee concerning the information and materials given out by organizations or content found at websites, and we are not responsible for any changes that occur after this book's publication. If you find an error, please contact Prufrock Press Inc.

Prufrock Press Inc.
P.O. Box 8813
Waco, TX 76714-8813
Phone: (800) 998-2208
Fax: (800) 240-0333
http://www.prufrock.com

TWISTED TRUE TALES FROM SCIENCE

INSANE INVENTORS

STEPHANIE BEARCE

WITH ILLUSTRATIONS BY
ELIZA BOLLI

Prufrock Press Inc.
Waco, Texas

TWISTED TRUE TALES
FROM SCIENCE

INSANE INVENTORS

TABLE OF *Contents*

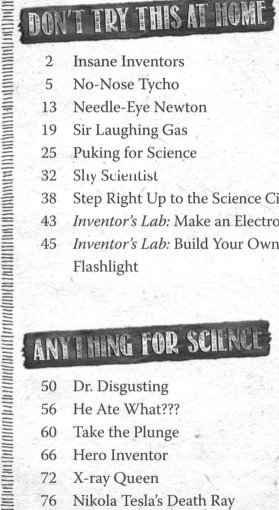

STRANGE DAYS OF SCIENCE

INSANE INVENTORS

"NECESSITY IS THE MOTHER OF INVENTION."
—OLD ENGLISH PROVERB

odern humans take inventions for granted. They sleep on a nice comfortable mattress, that isn't full of bugs and rodents, because inventors in the 1800s discovered that tightly packed cotton keeps out unwanted critters. They wake up with the help of an alarm clock, which was first built in 1300s Germany, and use a toothbrush to clean their teeth, rather than their finger, because of a patent from 1857.

They grab a slice of bread for toast, thanks to the invention of the bread slicer in 1924. Then they head to school or work in an automobile first invented by Karl Benz in 1846.

The truth is that everything humans use had to be invented. Some inventions were logical, like putting a wooden handle on a shell to create a spoon. Others were accidents—like the invention of Ivory soap. (A worker left the mixer on too long and it filled the soap with air so it floated in water.) Other inventions took years of research and testing, like the search for a polio vaccine. But everything we use was created from the experimentation and imagination of another human being.

Sometimes inventors have to do dangerous experiments to figure out whether their idea will work or not. Often, rather

Just a few inventions	
1300s	Alarm clock
1800s	Mattress
1846	Automobile
1857	Toothbrush
1924	Bread slicer

than endanger someone else, the inventor experiments on him- or herself. It can mean jumping off a tall building holding a bunch of cloth and ropes to test the idea of a parachute. It can mean injecting yourself with poison to study the effectiveness of an antidote. It can even mean dying while testing the invention of a submarine or a diving suit.

Regular people look at these inventors and think, "They've got to be insane." Only a crazy person would volunteer to drink vomit to see how disease spreads or test the effects of strange gasses by breathing them. Only an insane woman would sleep with radioactive radium by her bed. Only a crazy man would use his own body as a crash test dummy. But these scientists and inventors risked their lives to make changes that would help all of humanity.

NO-NOSE TYCHO

Tycho Brahe was never wrong. At least that's what he believed. And he was willing to do anything to prove his point, including fighting a sword duel. It didn't go well.

Born in Skane, Denmark in 1546, Brahe was one of a pair of twin boys born to Beate Bille and Otte Brahe. Brahe's twin brother died shortly after his

> Tycho Brahe was never wrong. At least that's what he believed. And he was willing to do anything to prove his point, including fighting a sword duel.

birth, but Brahe survived and lived with his parents until he was 2 years old. When he was still a toddler, Brahe was kidnapped by his father's brother.

Uncle Jørgen was a Vice-Admiral and quite wealthy. He was also childless. Jørgen claimed that he had made a deal with Brahe's father before he was born, that Brahe would be given to Jørgen to raise. Brahe's father reneged on the deal. Jørgen said he was only taking what was rightfully his. And because Tycho was going to be named Uncle Jørgen's only heir, Brahe's parents eventually agreed to let Jørgen and his wife raise Brahe.

Education became the central focus of Brahe's life. He began studying Latin when he was 7 years old and entered the University of Copenhagen when he was 13. His uncle wanted Tycho to become a lawyer, but Brahe was fascinated with the stars and heavens. During his first year at university, there was a solar eclipse, and Brahe became fascinated with how scientists of the time had accurately predicted the time of the eclipse. He spent all of his spare time and much of his study time learning all he could about the constellations.

When he turned 16, Uncle Jørgen decided that it was time for Brahe to get serious about his law studies. He hired a 20-year-old tutor named Anders Vedel and sent the two young men off to Leipzig, Germany.

But Brahe was determined that he was going to become an astronomer. He bought expensive instruments and books and stayed up late at night to study the stars. He hid these from his tutor and did very poorly in his law studies. His uncle was furious, but Brahe didn't care. He was studying what he wanted and thought his uncle was wrong to force him to study law.

At 17, Brahe was observing a special celestial event where Jupiter and Saturn passed very close to each other. He was aghast when he found out that the astronomers' predictions were off by several weeks. Brahe believed he could do better and began working on much more precise observations.

He completely stopped his law studies and dedicated himself to perfect observation of the exact position of the stars and planets. His tutor gave up trying to teach him and left, but the two remained good friends for life. His uncle was not pleased that Brahe refused to study law, and his visit home in May of 1565 was probably full of family arguments. But the arguments stopped a month later: His uncle died of pneumonia after rescuing the king of Denmark from drowning. As his uncle's only heir, Brahe became a very, very rich young man.

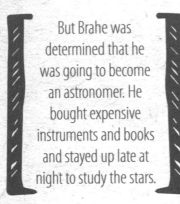

But Brahe was determined that he was going to become an astronomer. He bought expensive instruments and books and stayed up late at night to study the stars.

He no longer had to listen to anybody tell him what he could and could not study. He devoted himself to learning the mathematics needed to study celestial objects and studied with famous astronomer Bartholomew Schultz.

During this time, Brahe got into an argument with another student about who was the better mathematician. As usual, Brahe was sure he was the best. To settle the argument, the two agreed to have a sword duel—in the dark. Brahe may have been better at math, but he was not the best at dueling. During the fight, Brahe's nose was sliced off his face. For the rest of his life, Brahe wore a prosthetic nose that was made of metal. He carried putty with him to keep the nosepiece glued to his face.

Although he may have been conceited about his abilities, it was somewhat justified. Brahe made the most accurate celestial observations of his time and challenged the scientific beliefs of the period. For example, he studied a strange light that was in the sky in 1572. His accurate calculations proved that this was

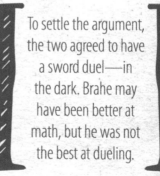

To settle the argument, the two agreed to have a sword duel—in the dark. Brahe may have been better at math, but he was not the best at dueling.

not a simple atmospheric phenomenon, as astronomers of the day thought. We now know that Brahe made the first accurate study of a supernova.

Brahe became famous for his scientific work, and the king of Denmark awarded him his own island to continue his studies of the heavens. For the next 20 years, Tycho lived in his own scientific castle that had the most sophisticated astronomy tools of the day. He had a chemistry lab in his basement and a printing press to print his books exactly as he wanted. He threw huge parties that were attended by nobility from around the world.

But in the late 1590s, Brahe got into an argument with the new king of Denmark. He packed up his laboratory and moved to Prague. In 1599, he became the royal mathematician for the Emperor of Prague. He took on an assistant named Johannes Kepler and worked on theories of planetary motion.

Brahe died in 1601, and his pride probably contributed to his death. He died 11 days after dining at the royal palace. During the party, he drank a great deal of wine, but refused to get up to go to the bathroom because he believed it was inappropriate etiquette. When he got home, he could not urinate and in the next few days, he developed a fever and excruciating intestinal pain and died.

After his death, Kepler used Brahe's notes and observations to deduce the three laws of planetary motion. Kepler's theories laid the groundwork for the work of scientist Sir Isaac Newton.

IF YOU GIVE A MOOSE TO TYCHO BRAHE . . .

Who would have a moose for a pet? Tycho Brahe, of course. He didn't just have the moose wandering around on the lawn or in a pen, though. He invited the moose inside and showed it off at parties. He let the moose stroll through the living rooms and in the ballroom. Imagine having to dance around a huge moose! Imagine the poor servants who had to clean up after moose "accidents!" That had to be one stinky job.

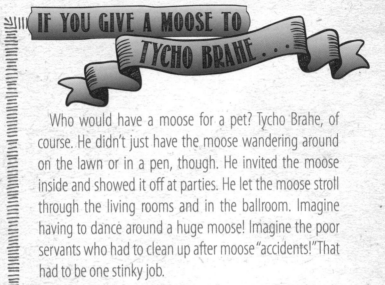

NEEDLE-EYE NEWTON

The legend is that Isaac Newton was sitting under an apple tree in 1666, just minding his own business, when a piece of fruit hit him on the head. And BOOM! He discovered the laws of gravity. That's not quite how it happened.

For certain, the apple never hit him on the head. That part was made up years after Newton died. But nobody is sure the event actually ever happened at all. Newton only started telling the story when he was an old man, long after he had become famous for inventing calculus, building a better telescope, and discovering the laws of motion. He thought it made an amusing story to help explain his theories.

One story Newton did not share with audiences was how he did his research on light and color. He was interested in how the eye worked and how it saw color, so he decided that the best way to do this was to push a needle into his own eye. Then, like any good scientist, he wrote about the results of the experiment.

> For certain, the apple never hit him on the head. That part was made up years after Newton died. But nobody is sure the event actually ever happened at all.

This experiment took place when Newton was 23 years old. He had been studying at Cambridge University when plague broke out in London. In just a few months, thousands of people had died. The professors at Cambridge were afraid that visitors would bring the plague to the university, so they closed down the school. Newton and the other students went home. Some never returned because they caught the horrible fever in their hometown and died. But Newton went to the solitude of his country home and never got sick. Instead, he spent his time experimenting, including poking a needle in his eye.

Newton wrote in his science journal that he slid the bodkin (a blunt needle) between the eyeball and the bone and pushed it back as far as he could to the backside of his eye. He observed that having the needle in his eye caused him to see "several white and dark-colored circles."

He continued to experiment to see the difference between having a needle in his eye in a light room and a dark room. In a light room, he said the circles were bluish. He still wasn't done and also tried the same experiment with a "sharp" bodkin. He found that when he moved the needle or bodkin, spots appeared, but when he stopped moving the needle, the spots disappeared. He also experimented with looking directly at the sun. He used the results of his experiments to write an essay titled "Of Colours."

Amazingly, Newton did not seriously damage his eyes with his experiments. He went on to experiment with prisms and eventually discovered how to make a telescope using mirrors instead of heavy lenses. He was able to create a more powerful microscope that was 10 times smaller than traditional telescopes. The scientists in the Royal Society were impressed and asked Newton to share the results of his research with them.

But Newton wasn't big on sharing information. He liked to keep discoveries to himself, so he gave a vague description of his experiments. When the scientists questioned him about his methods, Newton got angry and picked a fight with the head of the Royal Society. It started a lifelong battle between scientist Robert Hooke and Isaac Newton that didn't end until Hooke's death.

He continued to experiment to see the difference between having a needle in his eye in a light room and a dark room.

Newton was good at making people angry. He fought with Gottfried Leibniz over who actually invented calculus. When Leibniz published his work, Newton threw a fit and said he'd done the work 20 years before. Of course, Newton had never bothered to publish his work so no one knew he'd come up with calculus. It was only when Leibniz was getting the glory that Newton bothered to show his work.

> Newton was good at making people angry. He fought with Gottfried Leibniz over who actually invented calculus.

Newton really didn't want to share credit with Leibniz. In 1713, the Royal Society formed a committee to solve the question of who invented calculus. The committee declared that Newton had beaten Leibniz by two decades. But the author of the Royal Society report was actually Sir Isaac Newton. Their feud also lasted until death. Historians now believe that Newton and Leibniz independently invented the process of calculus, but Newton did indeed discover it 20 years earlier.

NEWTON'S GOLD?

As Isaac Newton grew older, it is said he became a little crazy. He was obsessed with studying the philosopher's stone. Yup—the same stone that is in the Harry Potter books. (Of course, Newton never knew about Harry Potter.) Newton was sure he could find a way to turn lead into gold and create his own philosopher's stone.

When Newton died, hundreds of his papers written on alchemy were found, but friends of Newton hid the papers to protect the great scientist's reputation. The papers were later found and sold at an auction in 1936.

Modern-day scientists have studied samples of Newton's hair and found that it contains huge amounts of mercury. Mercury poisoning often leads to insanity. The exposure to mercury was probably the result of years of unprotected experiments.

SIR LAUGHING GAS

The day after Christmas in 1799, Sir Humphry Davy stripped off his shirt, stuck a thermometer under his armpit, and stepped into an airtight box. His goal? To find out how long he could breathe nitrous oxide (laughing gas) without passing out. Sounds like a laugh, doesn't it?

This young English scientist had been experimenting with nitrous oxide for several months.

He set up a chemical reaction by heating nitrate of ammoniac and catching the escaping gas in a bellow (a thick cloth bag). Then he breathed in the gas to see what effect it would have on him. Lucky for Davy, the gas was not lethal. Instead of dying, he felt giddy and happy. He wrote in his reports that the gas made him feel like laughing and dancing.

When he told some of his fellow scientists about the gas, they quickly agreed to help Davy with his experiments. Davy invited friends to come to his laboratory in the evening and breathe from his bag of gas. Their job was to write down their observations on how the gas made them feel. They all felt very happy and the vapor was nicknamed "laughing gas."

> Lucky for Davy, the gas was not lethal. Instead of dying, he felt giddy and happy. He wrote in his reports that the gas made him feel like laughing and dancing.

Soon word leaked out about Davy and his laughing gas. People invited him to parties where he brought his bag of gas and guests took turns inhaling the fumes. None of the people seemed to suffer any long-term consequences, but several of them did breathe in so much that they lost consciousness.

Davy believed his discovery of laughing gas needed deeper scientific research. He hoped that he might be able to find a way to use laughing gas as a chemical anesthetic for surgery. It seemed like it would be a good alternative to the current method of a shot of whiskey and straps to hold the patient down.

When he stepped inside the sealed box that day after Christmas, he was going to see just how much laughing gas his body could withstand. His lab assistant pumped in four quarts of nitrous oxide. It was more than any living person had ever breathed. Just before he lost consciousness, Davy reported feeling that the world was brighter, his hearing was better, and he saw "shining packets of light and energy."

He woke up when his assistant dragged him out of the box and removed the nitrous oxide tube from his mouth. Breathing fresh air, he fully recovered, and that week he began writing a 580-page report to the Royal Society. The Society was impressed with his report on the new gas, but it didn't become popular with doctors until the 1860s because it was difficult to process and store the gas. It did, however, become popular with the public, and many people had laughing gas parties where the whole group would breathe in the gas and watch each other's antics. Because it was a gas, people didn't think it was as wicked as getting drunk on alcohol. The laughing gas fad eventually faded away, and nitrous oxide became a tool of the medical profession.

Experimenting on himself with nitrous oxide was just the first of many discoveries Humphry Davy made for science. Davy became fascinated with electricity and began experimenting with chemicals and the effect of electric charges. He discovered the elements sodium, calcium, and potassium. He continued to test chemicals on himself throughout his career, and eventually his health suffered from his experiments. He damaged his eyesight in experiments with nitrogen trichloride

> When he stepped inside the sealed box that day after Christmas, he was going to see just how much laughing gas his body could withstand.

(an explosive chemical compound) and hired a lab assistant named Michael Faraday to help him. Faraday built on Davy's experiments and helped discover principles that led to the development of generators, electric motors, and refrigeration.

BEN AND THE AIR BATH

Benjamin Franklin is known for the invention of bifocals, the Franklin Stove, the odometer, and the lightning rod. He did all this while helping to found the United States of America. How did Franklin get so much energy and great ideas? Franklin attributed it to his healthy habits of swimming for exercise and taking a daily air bath.

Every morning, Franklin would get up and strip out of his nightclothes, down to nothing at all. Then, he would throw the windows open and take an "air bath" for about an hour. He believed that fresh air on the skin was healthy. He often spent time in his room writing letters or reading in his birthday suit. Franklin did not usually receive visitors during his air bath time.

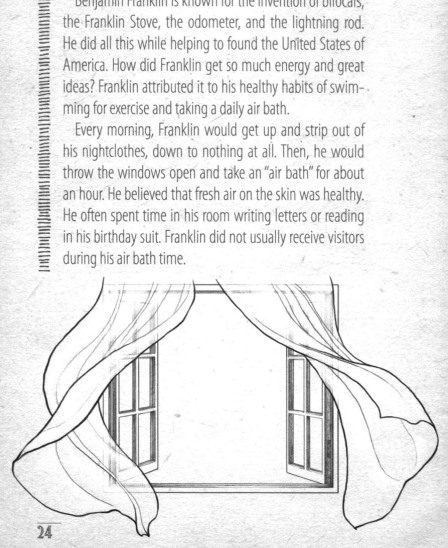

PUKING FOR SCIENCE

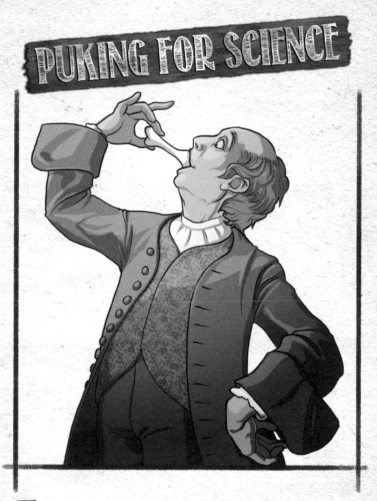

Lazzaro Spallanzani was always curious. He wondered how language was created, and how nature worked. Why could salamanders and tadpoles regrow their tails, but cats could not? Where did springs and fountains come from? How do plants grow? And what happens to food when people eat it?

In the mid-1700s, there were no X-rays. Nobody had invented microscopic cameras or ultrasound. The only way for a scientist to see inside a body was to cut it open, and there really weren't many volunteers for that. Spallanzani realized that when it came to studying human digestion, he was going to have to use himself as the test subject.

As a professor of natural history, Spallanzani was famous for his daring experiments. He had climbed the Italian mountains to prove that snowmelt contributed to springs and rivers. He had figured out how to aim sunbeams at salamanders so he could see their blood flow through a microscope, and he had experimented with animals and their digestive systems.

Spallanzani had fed glass balls to chickens and turkeys and learned that their powerful grinding gizzard could turn the glass into sand in just a few hours. He created tin tubes with small holes punctured in them, so he could learn what happened to food that was eaten by animals. He wanted to see if the juices in the stomach dissolved the food or if it was ground up like in birds.

After he filled the tube with food, Spallanzani poked the tube down the animal's throat and waited for it to be expelled in the animal's manure. Then he fished the tube out of the animal dung and opened the tube to see what was left inside.

> Spallanzani had fed glass balls to chickens and turkeys and learned that their powerful grinding gizzard could turn the glass into sand in just a few hours.

Getting the animals to swallow the tubes was not easy. He was attacked by birds when they fought back and was bitten by both dogs and snakes. Spallanzani knew it would be even more difficult to get a human to cooperate with the experiment, so he tested himself.

He started his human digestive experiments by chewing a piece of bread and spitting it back out. He took the chewed-up bread and put it into a small linen sack. He sewed the sack shut and then swallowed it. About 23 hours later, Spallanzani fished the sack out of his own fecal matter. He found that the sack was not damaged in any way, but the bread had vanished.

Since he hadn't had any digestive issues swallowing the bag of bread, he decided to go ahead with more experiments. Spallanzani carved tiny capsules out of wood. Like the tin tubes he used on animals, these had holes that allowed the digestive juices to reach the food inside. If the food disappeared in the wood capsules, this would tell Spallanzani that food was being dissolved by digestive juices rather than by the smashing action of the stomach.

Once again, he found the capsule came out the other end of his body in about 23 hours. The capsule was whole and had not been damaged, but the food inside had dissolved. Food was being digested by the juices in the stomach. It was the first scientific proof of how human digestion worked.

But Spallanzani wasn't done experimenting. He was still curious. What could the stomach juices dissolve? He filled the capsules with tough meat and gristle. He had to dig that capsule out of his fecal matter and reswallow it three times before the gristly meat disappeared, but eventually the stomach juices did dissolve it.

Then, he tried a piece of bone. Even after he swallowed and digested it several times, the bone did not dissolve. He decided that humans should avoid eating bones.

Next, he wanted to try experiments with the gastric juices outside of the body. He had gotten gastric juice from animals by forcing them to swallow a sponge and then pulling the sponge back up. He wrung the juice out of the sponge.

He tried the same experiment on himself, but he could only swallow two sponges at a time and they didn't soak up enough liquid for him to experiment with. Finally, he decided to try vomit.

He woke up early in the morning, when he was sure his stomach was empty, and stuck his finger far down his throat. This caused an automatic gag response and he threw up gastric juice. He used this juice in several experiments and learned that gastric juice would reduce a piece of meat to slime in just 3 days.

Because of Spallanzani's experiments, scientists understood for the first time that humans grind their food with their teeth, but there is no more grinding done once food is swallowed. The rest of the digestive process is completed through chemical reactions.

His experiments in digestion ended in about 1778, but that was by no means the end of his scientific career. Spallanzani kept experimenting the rest of his life. He tested the theories of regeneration by cutting off the tails of salamanders and tadpoles and observing how they grew back. He studied the speed of lava flowing on Mount Vesuvius. He passed out from inhaling poisonous gasses on Mount Etna. He also experimented with the theories of spontaneous generation and helped prove that animals did not magically arise from dirt or water.

Then, he tried a piece of bone. Even after he swallowed and digested it several times, the bone did not dissolve. He decided that humans should avoid eating bones.

When he died at the age of 70, his brother had Spallanzani's heart removed, preserved in a marble jar, and donated it to his hometown parish. Spallanzani died of a bladder disease, so his brother also had the bladder preserved and gave it to the historical museum at the University of Pavia.

SHY SCIENTIST

Henry Cavendish loved his books. He adored his science laboratory. He hated people.

Born in 1731, Cavendish was a member of the English nobility. Both of his grandfathers were dukes, and Cavendish, as the oldest son, was expected to study at university to practice law. But Cavendish was so shy that he had trouble talking to his family. Arguing law in front of strangers was more frightening than he could imagine.

Cavendish left school without getting a degree and set up a laboratory at his father's estate where he spent most of his time. For the next 40 years, Cavendish did research on an amazing number of scientific principles. With primitive tools and no calculator, he accurately estimated that the Earth weighed 6 billion trillion metric tons. Today's scientists have used space-age technology and hyperfast computers to calculate that the weight of the Earth is 5.9725 billion trillion metric tons. Cavendish's calculations were amazing.

He also experimented with chemistry and became the first scientist to ever isolate the element hydrogen. After that, he combined hydrogen and oxygen to form water in the laboratory. His research was nearly 100 years ahead of other sci-

entists', but many of his discoveries were not credited to him until nearly 60 years after his death. He was so shy that he didn't want to publish his work. He took decades of meticulous scientific notes and never shared his discoveries with any other scientists.

The bulk of his work was published by James Clerk Maxwell. In the 1870s, Maxwell went through Cavendish's volumes of notes and discovered that the shy scientist had discovered the principles of electrical conductivity, the law of partial pressures, and the science of thermodynamics. If his work had been shared with the world, science could have made greater strides at an earlier age.

> His research was nearly 100 years ahead of other scientists', but many of his discoveries were not credited to him until nearly 60 years after his death. He was so shy that he didn't want to publish his work.

But Cavendish was so shy that he rarely spoke to other people. His only social outings were to attend the weekly scientific dinner of the Royal Society. But if anyone wanted to ask him a question, they were told that they should not talk to him directly. To try to get an answer from him, people were advised to quietly walk over to where he was standing and talk to the air. Never address him to his face. If Cavendish was in a good mood, he might mumble a scientific answer. If not, he would just walk away.

Cavendish was quite wealthy and could afford to hire staff to take care of his household needs, so he did not have to talk to shop people or repairmen. He even built a private staircase in his house so he could avoid running into his housekeeper. He was especially scared of women and would leave instructions for his housekeeper on a piece of paper.

He never got over his extreme shyness. When he died in 1810 at the age of 78, Henry left the world a wealth of scientific knowledge and a fortune that today would be worth more than $730 million.

ANOTHER SHY GUY

Gregor Mendel was another inventor who was quiet and shy. Known as the father of genetics, Mendel was a monk who enjoyed working in his garden. He was so shy that he twice failed his oral exams at school. Explaining answers out loud made him nervous. But he loved to write and took meticulous notes on his observations on plant breeding. He coined the phrases *recessive* and *dominant genes*, and in 1865, published a paper about his work. But nobody took a serious look at the quiet scientist's work.

Mendel died just 3 years later and his work was largely ignored for 30 years. In 1900, four scientists redis-covered Mendel's work, and the invention of modern-day genetics was finally brought to light.

STEP RIGHT UP TO THE SCIENCE CIRCUS

ressed in the formal suits and dresses of 1798, the audience was quiet. Barely a whisper could be heard as Professor Giovanni Aldini took the stage. In front of him was the body of a freshly killed ox. The head had been removed before it was placed on the table. Aldini explained to audience members that they were going to see a demonstration of animal electricity—proof that animal bodies contained electricity and that electricity could control the body.

Aldini took two metal rods and hooked them to a battery. He touched one rod to the dead animal and nothing happened. But when he touched the second rod, one of the animal's legs moved as if it was alive. The audience screamed. Was Aldini some sort of resurrectionist trying to make the dead come back to life? Aldini moved the rods to a different spot and made another leg move. People were horrified and amazed. And they always kept coming back for more. Aldini put on his science shows all across Europe—almost like a traveling science circus. But he wasn't just trying to scare people to death, he was raising money to study galvanism.

Barely a whisper could be heard as Professor Giovanni Aldini took the stage. In front of him was the body of a freshly killed ox. The head had been removed before it was placed on the table.

Giovanni Aldini was continuing the experiments his uncle Luigi Galvani had started in the 1780s. Galvani had learned that when a static spark touched a dead frog's leg, the leg would move. He began experimenting with other animal parts and found that they also reacted to electrical stimulation. The study of electricity in animals was called *galvanism* in honor of Galvani. But rival scientist Alessandro Volta (inventor of the electric battery) thought Galvani's ideas were wrong and that the movement of the animal's dead body was due to the electric current in the cable. Not the animal.

After his uncle Luigi's death, Aldini took up the study of galvanism and continued experiments with birds, mammals, and even on human corpses. In 1803, the magistrates of London awarded Aldini the freshly executed body of George Forster for the purpose of experimentation. Aldini performed his gruesome experiments on Forster before an audience of London doctors, scientists, and wealthy citizens. He was successful in showing that the body would move when given electrical stimulation, and the audience was amazed and terrified.

Modern scientists now realize that the human body generates electricity through chemical reactions. The heart uses electrical current to keep beating. But in 1803, electricity was a new discovery and scientists were looking for ways to use it. Many thought that electricity could be used for medicinal purposes. Professor Aldini was one of those scientists and eventually experimented with using electricity to help cure mental illness.

Today's doctors do use electroconvulsive therapy to treat some severe forms of mental depression, but only after other medications have failed. Electrical stimulation is also used to revive heart attack patients, and electrical nerve stimulation is used help manage pain and repair damaged tissue.

Galvani had learned that when a static spark touched a dead frog's leg, the leg would move.

INSPIRATION FOR FRANKENSTEIN?

Some historians believe that author Mary Shelley had read about Aldini's experiments in galvanism and this was part of her inspiration for the story of Frankenstein. The observers of Aldini's experiments with the human corpse said it looked like he had "brought the man back to life." In reality, the electricity made the muscles contract. But Mary Shelley used her imagination to explore what might happen if a scientist were able to use electricity to bring a corpse back from the dead.

Inventor's Lab

MAKE AN ELECTROMAGNET

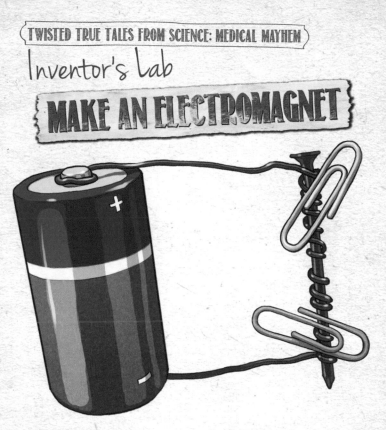

lectricity has fascinated inventors for centuries. You can experiment with electricity, too—all you need are simple materials.

MATERIALS

- » A large nail—about 3 inches long
- » 3–4 feet of plastic-covered copper wire
- » A new D-size battery
- » Some paper clips or other small metal objects
- » Gloves

Leave about 8 inches of wire loose at one end and wrap most of the rest of the wire around the nail. Try not to overlap the wire. Cut the wire (if needed) so that there is about another 8 inches loose at the other end, too. Strip off the plastic at each end of the wire.

Wear your gloves for the next part—the battery and metal get hot!

Attach one wire to one end of the battery and the other wire to the other end of the battery. You have just created an electromagnet! Put the point of the nail near a few paper clips, and it should pick them up!

Electromagnets run on electricity. The electricity flowing through the wire arranges the molecules in the nail so that they are attracted to certain metals.

Inventor's Lab

BUILD YOUR OWN FLASHLIGHT

MATERIALS

- » Cardboard tube
- » Copper wire with plastic coating (6–7 inches long)
- » Two D-cell batteries
- » Electrical tape
- » A flashlight lightbulb (2.2 or 3.0 volt)
- » 1 square of heavy dark paper cut slightly larger than the end of the cardboard tube
- » Paper cup with bottom cut out

First, strip the plastic coating off the end of the wire. Make sure you have at least 1/2 inch of exposed copper wire. Next, tape the paper over one end of the paper tube to form a bottom for your flashlight.

Use the electrical tape to secure one end of the wire to the bottom or negative end of the first battery. Make sure it's on tight. Then insert the battery with the wire taped to the end into the cardboard tube. Make sure you put the wired end in first so it sits at the bottom of the tube. Gently pull the wire up so that it sticks out the open end of the tube, and hold it against the wall of the tube.

Then, insert the second battery—make sure the negative end of the battery is down and touching the positive end of the first battery so there will be a complete electrical circuit.

Take the lightbulb to the top of the second battery. Make sure the metal bottom of the lightbulb is touching the positive post of the battery. Also, leave some of the metal on the side of the lightbulb exposed so that you can touch it with the wire.

Take the end of the wire that is poking out of the tube and touch it to the lightbulb. This should complete the electric circuit and the bulb will glow.

Tape the wire to the bulb. If you want to turn off the bulb, then just peel off the tape and move the wire away from the lightbulb.

Finally, tape the cup to the top of the tube to give your flashlight a cover.

Congratulations! You just built your own flashlight!

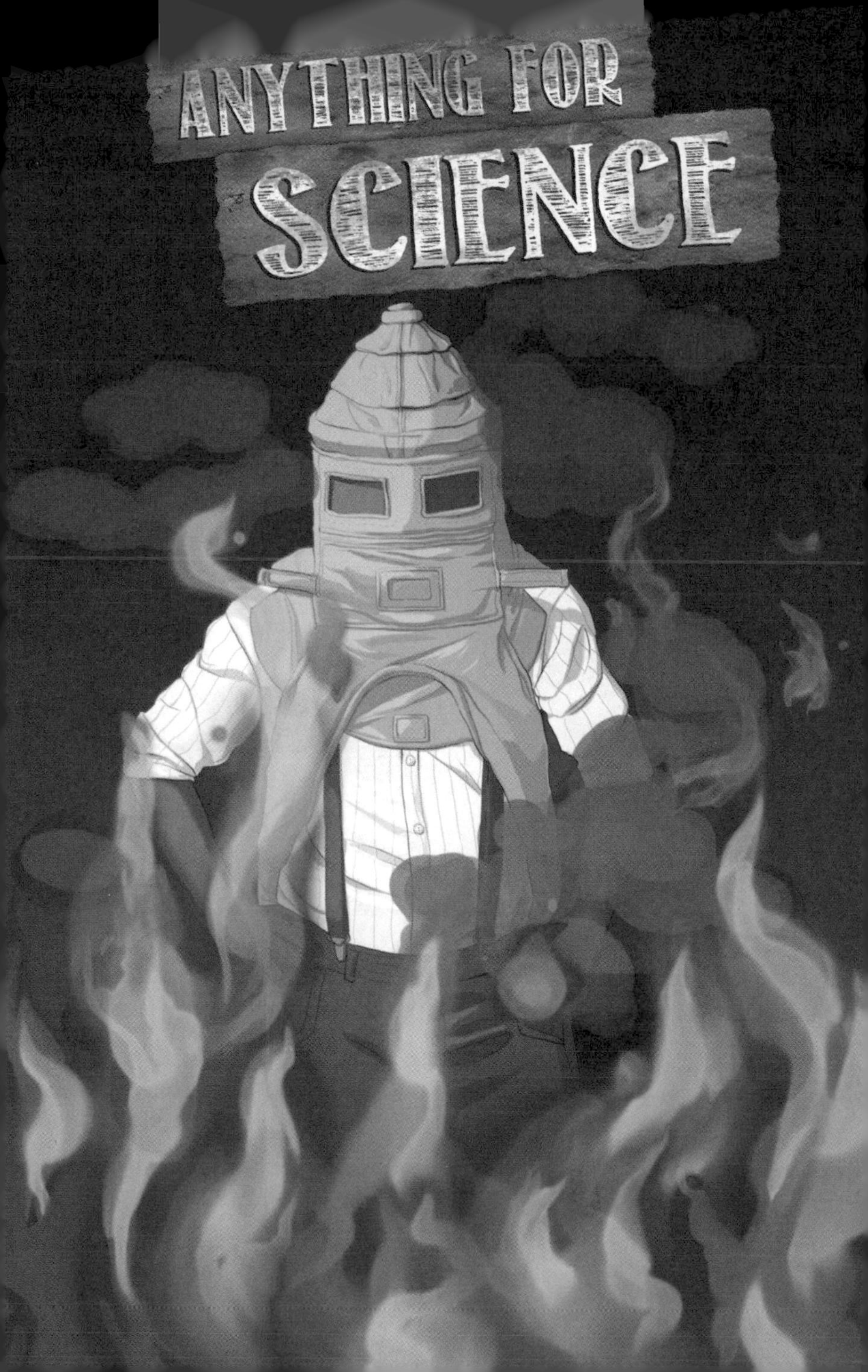
ANYTHING FOR
SCIENCE

DR. DISGUSTING

tubbins Ffirth was fascinated by a horrible disease called yellow fever. As a child, he witnessed the yellow fever epidemic of 1793 that killed thousands. He also saw the fever return every few summers. The victims of yellow fever suffered horrible deaths. Their bodies were racked by vomiting, their skin and eyes turned yellow, and before they died, they bled from their eyes and nose.

As a medical student at the University of Pennsylvania, Ffirth began a study in 1804 on the way yellow fever was transmitted. Ffirth, along with many other scientists, hoped that a cure could be invented for the horrible disease. But first, they had to learn how people contracted yellow fever.

Doctors of that time period thought that people caught yellow fever from "bad airs." They believed this because most of the outbreaks of yellow fever happened in the summer months when sewers and landfills smelled especially disgusting. Once a person had

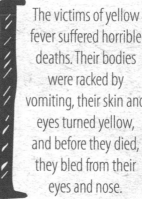

The victims of yellow fever suffered horrible deaths. Their bodies were racked by vomiting, their skin and eyes turned yellow, and before they died, they bled from their eyes and nose.

consumed the "bad airs" and taken ill, doctors believed that yellow fever spread quickly from one person to another.

But Ffirth believed that if yellow fever was really contagious and spread from one person to another, then the disease would not disappear in the winter months. And yellow fever was not a problem once it was cold enough for frost on the ground. Ffirth believed the first thing to research was if yellow fever was a contagious disease or not.

He set up experiments using animals as test subjects. Ffirth collected body fluids from yellow fever victims. He took saliva, blood, and vomit and fed these fluids to the animals. He also rubbed the fluids in cuts or sores on the animals and waited to see if any of the animals developed yellow fever. When none of them became ill, he concluded that either the animals were immune to yellow fever or it was not contagious.

Next Ffirth needed to conduct tests on humans. He knew that humans could get yellow fever, but he didn't want to risk the life of another person. Ffirth decided that the best way to study the disease was to experiment on himself. He collected more vomit, blood, urine, and saliva from yellow fever patients and proceeded to run the tests.

Ffirth made incisions on his arms and rubbed the fluids in the cuts. He did not become ill. He made a vapor tent over each fluid and inhaled the air from the bodily fluids. He still didn't get sick. Last, he had to find out if he could catch yellow fever by ingesting the fluids. So Stubbins Ffirth gave his all for science and proceeded to drink vomit, urine, and other bodily fluids from yellow fever patients. Amazingly, he did not get sick.

> Ffirth decided that the best way to study the disease was to experiment on himself. He collected more vomit, blood, urine, and saliva from yellow fever patients and proceeded to run the tests.

Ffirth wrote up his findings and presented them to the University of Pennsylvania and was awarded his medical degree. Although Ffirth did conduct his experiments correctly, what he did not comprehend was the idea that yellow fever might be trans-

MOSQUITO FEEDER

In 1900, when Dr. Walter Reed and his team of scientists were trying to figure out if mosquitos caused yellow fever, they needed a way to test their theory. Just like Stubbins Ffirth, they knew they could not risk the lives of other people, so the team experimented on themselves. They built a special tent where they could trap mosquitos infected with yellow fever. Then they went in the tent and voluntarily let the mosquitos feed on their bodies.

Three of the men became ill with yellow fever, and one man died. Reed was devastated that one of his men died during the experiment, but he was determined that his death would not be in vain. Reed continued with his work until he was able to identify the tiny parasite that caused yellow fever. It took the work of numerous brave researchers who were willing to self-experiment to uncover the secrets of yellow fever.

mitted by an insect. It would be almost 100 years later when Dr. Walter Reed began his famous 1901 studies on the relationship between mosquitos and yellow fever. It was not until the 1950s that a successful vaccine was invented for this disease.

HE ATE WHAT???

illiam Buckland loved collecting fossils. As a professor at Oxford, his living quarters were filled from floor to ceiling with samples of ammonites, fossilized bones, plants, and shells. One student made a visit to Buckland's rooms in 1824 and said there was only one rickety chair that was not covered with rocks or fossils. Buckland was the original dinosaur bone hoarder.

Buckland became famous for researching and writing about giant fossilized lizard bones that he named *Megalosaurus*. It was Buckland's writing that popularized the term *dinosaur*. And it was Buckland who encouraged students to study the ancient fossils by giving vivid lectures about what he believed life was like in prehistoric times.

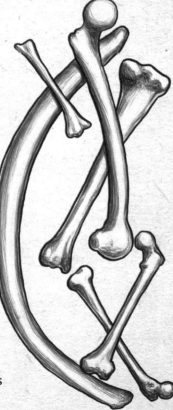

Every part of dinosaur life interested him, but he was especially fascinated by dinosaur feces (poop). Breaking open the fossilized feces, Buckland was able to learn about what the ancient animals ate and develop theories about prehistoric food chains. Buckland believed that the stomach was what ruled the world. Animals had to eat to stay alive, and hunger was a primary drive in nature.

Buckland himself was fascinated with eating and claimed it was his goal to eat everything in the animal kingdom. And he meant *everythin*g. He tasted all of the animals common to England, such as mice, hedgehogs, badgers, snakes, and bats. Then, he decided to start cooking more exotic animals. Friends and colleagues who went to dinner at Buckland's home could never be sure what they were eating. He served elephant trunk, crocodile, horse's tongue, sliced porpoise head, and rhino meat. If he could catch it, Buckland would eat it.

He wasn't picky, but did tell people that the taste of mole was repulsive and he gagged while eating a bluebottle fly. People wondered why in the world he wanted to taste so many strange animals. Perhaps he was just adventurous, or maybe he considered it research for the eating habits of the prehistoric animals he loved. Why did he want to eat every type of animal? It's a mystery (one no one's quite daring enough to solve for themselves!).

> Buckland himself was fascinated with eating and claimed it was his goal to eat everything in the animal kingdom.

It is documented that Buckland was always willing to taste anything at any time. Once, when he was touring a cathedral, he was shown a dark spot on the floor. The legend was that the dark spot was the holy blood of a saint. Buckland dropped to his knees and licked the floor. He stood up and told the tour guide that it was not blood but bat urine. The cathedral had bats roosting in the roof. Nobody asked Buckland how he recognized the taste of bat urine.

The most astonishing story of Buckland was told by writer Augustus Hare. He claimed that Buckland was visiting Lord Harcourt's home just outside of Oxford. Lord Harcourt was showing his dinner guests one of his many treasures. He passed around a small silver casket and claimed that it held the dried heart of King Louis XVI. When the casket reached Buckland, he told the group he'd never eaten a king's heart. Before anyone could stop him, he popped the heart in his mouth and it was gone—lost to Buckland's digestive system.

Despite his crazy eating habits, Buckland lived to be 72 years old. He died in Oxford in 1856.

TAKE THE PLUNGE

efore 1852, nobody wanted to ride in an elevator. Elevators were death traps with ropes that could snap any second and send riders plunging to their death. Lifts were considered too dangerous for humans and were only used to haul freight up and down in mines or factories. Sometimes workers were forced to ride in the elevators to assist in moving the freight. But it was a nerve-racking ride. The newspapers were full of stories of workers who had plummeted to their deaths when the rope broke.

In the 1850s, the world was changing rapidly. The Industrial Revolution, with its steam-powered engines, had made it possible to build taller buildings. The new buildings could be more than 10 stories high, but nobody wanted to walk up that many flights of stairs or haul boxes and furniture up that high. If only someone could make a safe elevator . . .

Elisha Otis was just the man for the job. As a master

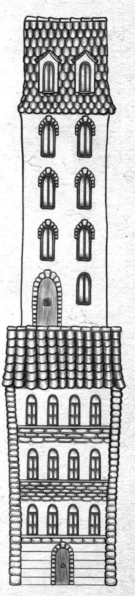

Elisha Otis, 1886

mechanic for O. Tingley & Company, he had already invented an automatic turner that made bedsteads 4 times faster than could be done by hand. He also invented a railway safety brake that could be controlled by the train engineer. He even had plans for an automatic bread-making oven.

Otis was put in charge of cleaning up an old sawmill in Yonkers, NY. His job was to turn it into a new bedstead factory that would use his automatic turner system. But he had to figure out a way to get all of the heavy machinery to the upper levels of the old building. None of the workers were willing to use an elevator or lift system. They were terrified the heavy equipment would break the ropes.

Otis thought about the problem and decided that the solution was to create an elevator brake just as he had invented a railway brake. He came up with an ingenious answer. He used a tough steel wagon spring meshing with a ratchet. If the rope broke, the spring would catch and hold the elevator.

He tested out his new invention by hauling all of the machinery to the upper levels of the old sawmill. Up and down, the lift hauled the heavy machinery. When a rope split, the wagon spring caught the elevator. His invention worked.

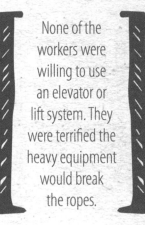

None of the workers were willing to use an elevator or lift system. They were terrified the heavy equipment would break the ropes.

Otis was excited. He had solved the problem of unsafe elevators. He patented his brake system and set up his own elevator company, sure that orders would come flying in. But there were no orders. Nobody believed that Otis had solved the problem. They were still afraid that getting in an elevator was a quick ride to death.

Then, Otis had another brilliant idea—a dangerous, but brilliant, idea. New York City was the site of the 1854 World's Fair. People from around the globe were in New York City learning about the latest and greatest inventions. Otis decided it was the perfect place to show off his elevator brake.

He had an elevator lift built inside the Crystal

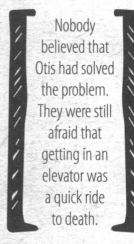

Palace Exhibit Hall. Then, he invited the world to come and see his live demonstration of his safety elevator. In front of a packed auditorium, Otis climbed onto the elevator platform. People stared as he turned on the steam motor and rose three stories above the audience. When Otis reached the top, his assistant pulled out an axe and dramatically cut the only rope holding the elevator.

Nobody believed that Otis had solved the problem. They were still afraid that getting in an elevator was a quick ride to death.

People screamed and covered their eyes, sure they were about to see Otis plummet to his death. Instead, the elevator jerked down a few inches, and then held firm. The elevator brake had worked. The crowd cheered.

The Otis Elevator was a hit. Orders poured into the company. Builders wanted elevators for their tall buildings. The Industrial Revolution was moving up into skyscrapers. The Otis Elevator Company became the world's largest manufacturer of elevators, escalators, and moving walkways. It is still in operation today, and most elevators still have a plaque inside that advertises the Otis name.

Elisha Otis never stopped inventing. He patented a steam plow in 1857, a rotary oven in 1858, and an oscillating steam engine in 1860. The creative inventor's life was cut short when he died from diphtheria in 1861 at the age of 49.

When Otis reached the top, his assistant pulled out an axe and dramatically cut the only rope holding the elevator.

HERO INVENTOR

arrett Morgan could fix just about anything. Broken sewing machines, busted motors, broken-down factory equipment—Morgan could fix it all. Morgan was a genius at figuring out how to make things better. While he was working as a sewing machine repairman, he invented a new belt fastener for sewing machines and got his first patent in 1912.

He did all of this with only a sixth-grade education, and during a time when American businesses were deeply prejudiced against people with dark skin color.

Morgan's parents were slaves until President Lincoln signed the Emancipation Proclamation in 1863. His father was the son of a slavemaster, John H. Morgan, and his slave mistress. Garrett Morgan's mother was half Native American and half African American. Morgan's race profoundly impacted his career and the success of his inventions.

Garrett Morgan could fix just about anything. Broken sewing machines, busted motors, broken-down factory equipment...

Despite prejudice against Black entrepreneurs, Morgan managed to successfully open his own sewing machine and shoe repair shop in 1907. By 1909, he had a shop with 32 employees and was making coats, suits, dresses, and other clothing. But Morgan wasn't just content to be a businessman. His active mind was still thinking of how to improve everything he saw.

He began to imagine a safety hood that could be used to help the firefighters breathe.

Morgan had seen local firefighters struggling to withstand the smoke of fires. He began to imagine a safety hood that could be used to help the firefighters breathe. He designed a canvas hood that had two tubes. One tube dangled near the floor to take advantage of the clean air beneath the smoke fumes. A wet sponge was used to filter out smoke and cool the air. He patented his invention in 1912. Two years later, he was ready to sell his safety hood and founded the National Safety Device Company.

But prejudiced investors did not want to purchase something invented by a Black man. Morgan had to have a White actor promote his safety hood so that people would buy it. Morgan was frustrated, but he wasn't willing to give up. He knew that his invention could save lives.

One night in 1916, Morgan was at his home in Cleveland when someone banged frantically on his door. The visitor had just come from a tunnel explosion under Lake Erie. Workers were trapped in the burning tunnel. Could Morgan come help and bring as many of his safety hoods as possible?

Morgan got his brother, Frank, out of bed. They didn't even bother to get dressed, but grabbed four safety hoods and went to the site of the explosion. When they arrived on the scene, the other rescue workers were skeptical. They didn't believe the safety hoods would work and weren't willing to try them.

Garrett Morgan

Garrett and Frank Morgan knew the hoods would work. They scrambled into the safety hoods and went into the smoke-filled tunnel. Within a few minutes they came back out carrying victims on their backs. They immediately went back in and rescued more people. The other workers were convinced and began taking turns going in and pulling out as many victims as they could. When they couldn't find any more survivors, they used the safety hoods to bring out the bodies of the dead so their families could bury them.

Sadly, Garrett and Frank Morgan were not recognized for their heroic efforts. Cleveland's newspapers totally ignored their role in providing the equipment or in the rescue of more than 20 people. Two White men, Thomas J. Clancy and Thomas Castleberry, were recognized as the "heroes" and given a $500 reward by the Carnegie Commission.

Despite this, news of Morgan's safety hood spread, and more than 500 cities bought hoods for use in their fire departments. He also sold the hoods to the U.S. Navy and Army, and they were used by the military during World War I.

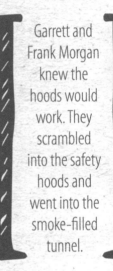

Garrett and Frank Morgan knew the hoods would work. They scrambled into the safety hoods and went into the smoke-filled tunnel.

Morgan became a successful businessman. He was the first Black man to own a car in Cleveland. He invented cosmetic products and also invented the first three-position traffic signal. His traffic signal regulated traffic better because it had a caution signal in addition to stop and go. He donated money to help fund scholarships for young Black students and worked tirelessly to help improve the treatment of Black people in America.

Garrett Morgan bringing first man out of the tunnel explosion under Lake Erie.

He died in 1963 at the age of 86. One month after his death, his achievements were recognized nationally during the centennial celebration of the Emancipation Proclamation.

X-RAY QUEEN

Everybody knows that X-rays are harmful to the human body. Well . . . at least everybody knows that now. In 1895, when Wilhelm Röntgen discovered he could use X-rays to take pictures of bone and internal organs, he had no idea that X-rays were any different than taking Kodak pictures. The world was amazed by pictures of delicate

hand bones and strong leg bones. Soon, everybody wanted to experiment with X-rays.

Elizabeth Fleischman was 28 years old when the news of Röntgen's invention reached the United States. She lived in the family home with her sister and brother-in-law, Dr. Michael Woolf. Fleischman had never finished high school because her family needed her to work to supplement the family income. But she was smart and liked to read, so even though she couldn't attend school, she kept on learning. She enjoyed numbers and worked as a bookkeeper for a company in San Francisco.

Fleischman was fascinated with the amazing new technology that allowed people to see inside the flesh of the hand to the bone. She wanted to experiment with photographs that pierced the veil of cotton and corsets and showed the skeleton and organs hidden beneath.

Fleischman also grasped the amazing implications that X-rays could have for medical purposes. Doctors could use X-rays to set broken bones, see ruptured intestines, and find shrapnel from gun-shots. Doctors could see inside the body without having to make incisions. It could be a powerful tool in surgery and medical research.

With the help of her brother-in-law, Fleischman set up one of the first X-ray laboratories in California. In 1900, the Spanish-American War was in full swing, and Fleischman was called upon to X-ray soldiers who had bullets and shrapnel lodged in their lungs and skulls. Her X-rays helped sur-geons know where to operate and saved countless lives.

Through her experiments, Fleischman discov-ered how to regulate the X-ray exposures to match tissue densities. She knew how to triangulate the location of the bullet and took photographic X-rays that led surgeons straight to the bullet. She was considered one of the best X-ray photographers in the world.

Sadly, she was also one of the first people to find out the horrible effects of exposure to X-rays. No studies had been done before allowing the public to work with X-rays. No one realized that X-rays damaged skin tissue, nervous systems, and caused cancer. After nearly 10 years of using X-rays to save other people's lives, Fleischman found her own life was in danger.

In 1905, Fleischman was diagnosed with advanced stage cancer in her arm. She had to have it amputated. But that treatment wasn't enough to save her life. She died from cancer just 7 months later.

Fleischman was one of many scientists who died from exposure to X-rays and radiation poisoning. Their deaths taught the world about the dangers of radiation. Now scientists realize that X-rays must be used with caution and people should have very limited exposure. X-ray technicians take precautions with their equipment and wear lead shields to limit their exposure. Fleischman's legacy is showing the world that when safely used, X-rays can be a powerful medical tool.

> After nearly 10 years of using X-rays to save other people's lives, Fleischman found her own life was in danger.

NIKOLA TESLA'S DEATH RAY

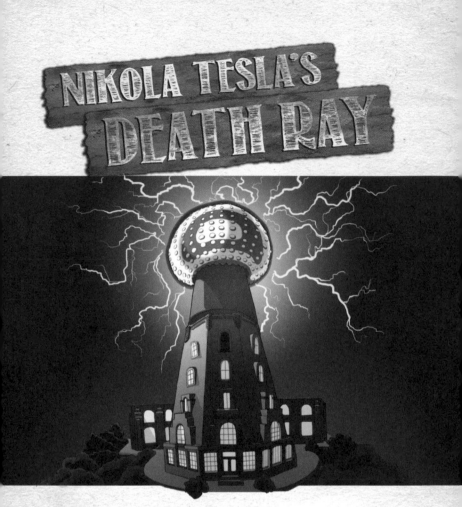

The reporter was shaking as he left the hotel. Could it be true? Could Nikola Tesla really have invented a death ray that could destroy 10,000 enemy airplanes from a distance of 250 miles? If President Roosevelt knew about this invention, then he could use it to protect America from war. The world could use it to stop all wars.

This was a miraculous discovery . . . if it was true.

After all, Tesla was an old man now. He had celebrated his 78th birthday on July 10, 1934. He spent his days feeding the pigeons of New York City. And talking to them. Maybe he was just plain bonkers. The reporter stopped to think. This was the man who had discovered alternating current. He had made electricity available to every home in the world. He held more than 700 patents. The man was a genius. The reporter ran for his office. Tesla inventing a death ray—this story was sure to sell newspapers.

Invention was as natural as breathing to Tesla. His mother was always inventing tools to help her with work around the house, and Tesla copied her example. When he was just 6, he invented his own frog hook and used it to bring home nice plump frogs for supper. He also invented a propeller that ran on the energy of June bugs. He attached four June bugs to

a small cross-shaped piece of wood. The wood balanced on a thin spindle. As the June bugs flapped their wings, the spindle rotated. Young Tesla considered his invention a success even if the June bugs weren't too happy about being subjects of his experiment. But his bug energy propeller was ruined when another little boy decided to make a snack of the June bugs. Tesla watched in gross amazement as the boy ate all four of his bugs like they were popcorn. Tesla never played with bugs again, and as he got older he refused to ever touch an insect.

Tesla had such a vivid imagination that as a child he suffered from what he called "visions." Sometimes he had trouble distinguishing the visions from real life, and they caused him to be depressed and frightened. But as he got older, Tesla said he learned how to control these visions and manipulate them to his advantage. His parents were both good at memorizing and encouraged Tesla to exercise his mind this way. He memorized poetry, long sonnets, and whole books. He could look at diagrams and remember every detail without ever seeing them again. He began picturing inventions in his mind in such detail that he would imagine the tiny gears and screws needed to build each part. He would test the invention in his mind until he was sure it would work in real life, and only then would he build a test model. The test models always worked.

Growing up in Serbia, Tesla attended the local schools and excelled in science and mathematics, but he was horrible in art class. His vivid imagination did not translate to paper, and Tesla never became good at drawing. Many of his inventions were never drawn out as plans. He simply built

Tesla's electromagnetic motor, 1888

them from the idea he had in his mind.

One of Tesla's first major inventions was an electromagnetic motor. It came to him in a vision. Like a flash before his eyes, he said he could see the motor. He was walking with a friend in the park, and he immediately picked up a stick and drew his idea in the dirt. He knew it would work and would revolutionize how electricity was distributed.

When Tesla immigrated to the United States he went to work for Thomas Edison. Edison was impressed with the younger man's ingenuity and asked Tesla if he could redesign the Edison company's direct current generators. He told Tesla, "There's $50,000 in it for you—if you can do it."

Tesla took the challenge, and in a few months, he showed up in Edison's office asking for his money. Edison told Tesla that he had only been "joking" and that he didn't understand American humor. Tesla was furious and immediately quit working for Edison. For the rest of their lives, Edison and Tesla were enemies.

Part of what angered Edison was Tesla's pure genius. Edison worked with a huge staff of scientists to develop his inventions, while Tesla was mostly a one-man show. Tesla received 300 patents for individually unique inventions. These inventions included the first radio-controlled boat, fluorescent lighting, alternating current electricity, and of course, the lightning-shooting Tesla Coil.

Tesla even had the idea for cell phones way back in 1901. He spent nearly 17 years working on a huge tower that was to be used for wireless telecommunications. It was being financed by millionaire J. P. Morgan. But when Morgan found out that the power created by the tower could not be metered and sold, Morgan pulled the funding. Tesla's dream of wireless communication died, and the world had to wait 60 years for cell phones to be invented.

With so many amazing inventions to his credit, the world was always anxious to learn what new ideas Tesla had cooked up. So when he announced that he had

> Tesla even had the idea for cell phones way back in 1901. He spent nearly 17 years working on a huge tower that was to be used for wireless telecommunications.

TESLA
THE LIGHTNING MAN

Tesla created the largest man-made lightning bolt. In 1899, he sent waves of seismic energy through the Earth to prove his theories about earthquake stations. As the energy rebounded, he added electricity and made a lightning bolt that was 130 feet high. The thunder was heard 22 miles away, and the meadow outside his Colorado laboratory glowed blue with the energy.

created a death ray, many people were sure he had. Others scoffed that Tesla was an old man who did nothing but feed pigeons and wander the streets mumbling to himself. He wasn't capable of inventing a death ray.

But when Tesla died in 1943 at the age of 86, the FBI ordered that all of his belongings be seized. Every one of his papers was taken and examined by the National Defense Research Committee. After reading the papers, the Defense Committee officially stated that Tesla's thoughts and efforts during his final years were primarily speculative.

Once Tesla died, his great ideas died with him. He was the only one capable of imagining a death ray, or cell phone, and then creating it. Other people needed detailed plans. Did Tesla have the ideas for a death ray? Probably. But like many of his other ideas, they needed his genius to complete them, and Tesla's imagination was so far ahead of his time that we are just now understanding his ideas.

QUIRKY GENIUS

Nikola Tesla had some odd quirks to his personality. He was obsessed with doing things in threes and would only stay in a hotel room that was divisible by the number 3. For the last 10 years of his life, he lived in room 3327 on the 33rd floor of the Hotel New Yorker.

He suffered from insomnia and claimed that he only slept for 2 hours a night, although sometimes he did take an afternoon nap. He hated jewelry, especially on women, and was so repulsed by human hair that he could not bear to touch it.

In his old age, he became obsessed with pigeons and spent hours feeding them and talking to them. Sometimes neighbors in his hotel would complain about the smell when he kept too many of them in his room.

MADAME CURIE FIGHTS A WAR

VOITURE RADIOLOGIQUE

> ### "ONE NEVER NOTICES WHAT HAD BEEN DONE; ONE CAN ONLY SEE WHAT REMAINS TO BE DONE."
> ### —MARIE CURIE

It was the fall of 1914, and the Great War was raging across France. A soldier lay on the stretcher groaning in pain. His back and legs showed the effects of shrapnel from mortar rounds. A nurse worked to calm him, while the doctor stood nearby talking to a small middle-aged woman sitting inside a truck.

The woman listened closely to the doctor and nodded. In a few minutes, the woman and doctor were unloading equipment from the truck. They pulled out one of the newfangled X-ray machines and began to scan the soldier's body.

The woman was the famous scientist Madame Marie Curie, and the truck carrying portable X-ray equipment was her brainchild. The two-time Nobel Prize-winning scientist wanted to help her adopted country, France, and she realized that X-rays were the best service she could provide. If she could get X-ray machines to the battlefield hospitals, then they would help doctors set broken bones and see bullets and shrapnel hidden in the body. But to do so would also be a dangerous mission. Madame Curie and anyone helping her would be in the direct line of fire. It was an experiment that could give life to soldiers, but death to Curie.

Marie Curie, 1920

Marie Curie convinced the government of France to name her the Director of the Red Cross Radiology Service.

Then she asked for donations of cars and money from wealthy friends. She took the cars and trucks to automobile body shops and had them transformed into vans that could haul her specially designed portable X-ray machines.

The grateful French soldiers started calling the mobile X-ray labs "petite Curies," and by October of 1914, there were 20 radiology vans on the battlefield. Curie herself trained radiological assistants to help on the front lines. Her first trainee was her 17-year-old daughter, Irène. Curie taught herself how to drive the vans and learned auto mechanics so she could do repairs when they broke down.

By 1916, Curie had established 200 stationary X-ray units and was training women as assistants at her Radium Institute. Over the course of the war, she trained 150 women who went to work at the war front.

After the war, Curie continued to invent new ways to use radium in helping the wounded. She began using a technique to collect a radioactive gas that was emitted from the radium.

By 1916, Curie had established 200 stationary X-ray units and was training women as assistants at her Radium Institute.

She worked alone using an electric pump to collect the gas in tiny glass tubes about a centimeter long. The gas was delivered to hospitals where the doctors placed the radioactive tube in platinum needles. Medical staff placed the needles in the patients' bodies where there was diseased tissue. It was radiation therapy on the battlefield.

The war ended in 1918, but Curie continued her war work for another year. She spent time teaching a group of American soldiers about radiology. Curie was never recognized for her work in the war effort, but her invention and innovation saved countless lives.

She is still best known for winning the Nobel Prize in Physics in 1903 and in Chemistry in 1911. But this groundbreaking woman was a person of many talents. She died in 1934 from aplastic anemia, a blood disease that is now known to result from too much exposure to radiation. She gave her life for science.

GLOWING PAPERS

Marie Curie and her husband Pierre did not realize how dangerous radioactive particles can be. Marie carried vials of polonium and radium in the pocket of her coat and stored them in her desk drawer. She even kept a little tube of polonium on her bedside table as a nightlight, because the radioactive material glowed in the dark.

Today Marie Curie's research papers, her lab notes, her furniture, and even her cookbooks are still radioactive. Her collections are housed at France's Bibliotèque Nationale. All the papers are stored in lead-lined boxes to protect visitors and workers from the effects of radiation. Anyone who wants to read her papers must wear a special suit that protects from radiation poisoning and sign a waiver of liability, stating he or she will not sue the library if he or she gets radiation sickness.

Inventor's Lab

GET GLOWING

Sir Isaac Newton experimented with his own eye to learn about human sight, but you can learn about how light works without poking your eye.

First, remember that black lights give off light that is ultraviolet, and human eyes cannot naturally see ultraviolet light. But phosphors absorb radiation and reflect it back as visible light. Petroleum jelly contains phosphors, so it will absorb the ultraviolet radiation and reflect it back in a form of light the human eye can see.

Use these materials to experiment with what makes things glow in the dark.

MATERIALS

- » A black light
- » Petroleum jelly
- » Piece of paper

Dip your finger in the petroleum jelly and write a word on the paper. When you are done, turn off the room light and turn on the black light. Can you see the light from the phosphors? Next, cover one hand in petroleum jelly and look at it under the black light.

Is there anything else you can find that glows under the black light? Often laundry detergents contain phosphors and may make white clothes glow in black light.

How can you use this new knowledge? Can you write secret notes to your friends? Plan a scary black light Halloween party?

Inventor's Lab

TRICK YOUR EYES

Are the horizontal lines sloping or straight?

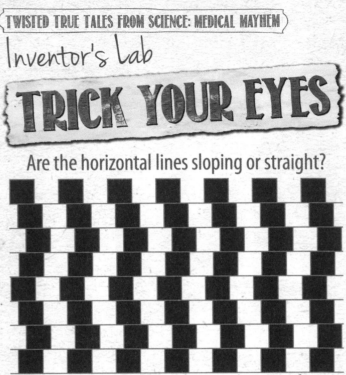

Answer: Straight

 ptical illusions trick the human eye into seeing something differently than it actually exists. Illusions use color, light, and patterns to create images that can be deceptive to our brains. Check out some of these optical illusions and see what your brain thinks.

1. https://kids.niehs.nih.gov/games/riddles/illusions

2. http://brainden.com/optical-illusions.htm

3. http://www.artistshelpingchildren.org/optical-illusions-eye-tricks-crafts.html

STRANGE DAYS
OF SCIENCE

THE AC/DC WAR

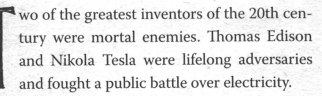

Two of the greatest inventors of the 20th century were mortal enemies. Thomas Edison and Nikola Tesla were lifelong adversaries and fought a public battle over electricity.

When Tesla arrived in America in 1884, he went to work for Thomas Edison. His job was to redesign the Edison company's direct current generators. Tesla believed that he would be paid $50,000 for the job. Edison said that he had been joking. Tesla never forgave Edison.

Tesla struck out on his own looking for investors, and in 1888 he struck a deal with George Westinghouse. Westinghouse purchased Tesla's patents for alternating electric current and went to work building electric plants and generators that would provide AC electricity throughout the United States.

AC electricity was in direct competition with Edison's DC, or direct current, method. In 1887, there were 1,212 Edison power stations in the United States providing electricity to business and homes. Edison had a virtual lock on the electricity business, and he liked it that way. But there was a problem with DC power. It was limited in how

Thomas Edison and Nikola Tesla were lifelong adversaries and fought a public battle over electricity.

far it could travel on wires before it began to lose power. This meant there had to be an electric plant built every mile to boost the energy. High-voltage alternating current could travel hundreds of miles without losing power. One station could be built to serve thousands of people. Businessmen quickly understood that the AC system would be much cheaper to construct.

Edison was determined to keep his DC electric business. He started a propaganda campaign against Tesla and Westinghouse, telling everyone that the stronger AC current was dangerous. AC current would kill people and burn down houses. He set up public shows where he put dogs, cows, horses, and even an elephant on stage. The animals were forced to step on a metal plate that was charged with AC. The animals were shocked by the AC current and died on stage, and the announcer told the audience that this would be the fate of anyone who touched alternating current.

Westinghouse and Tesla were furious. They knew that their alternating current could be safely used in homes and businesses, but electricity was a new invention. The general public had no idea how it worked. They were willing to believe Edison's demonstrations.

CENTENNIAL LIGHT BULB

In the United States, the average incandescent light bulb (that is, a bulb heated with a wire filament) has a lifespan of about 1,000 to 2,000 hours.

But dangling from the ceiling of a Livermore, California firehouse is a bulb that's burned for more than 989,000 hours——115 years. Since its first installation in 1901, it has rarely been turned off and has been proclaimed the "Eternal Light" by General Electric experts and physicists around the world. Began at 60 watts, it currently shines at 4 watts.

Tracing the origins of the bulb—known as the Centennial Light—raises questions as to whether it is a miracle of physics, or a sign that new bulbs are weaker. Its longevity still remains a mystery.

Then, Edison sponsored the construction of an electric chair that used AC current to execute a convicted murderer. He bargained that if he could get AC current associated with executions, then people would want nothing to do with the AC current.

But the truth won out, because AC current actually was the best solution for transmitting electric current over wires for long distances. In 1893, Westinghouse and Tesla won the contract to light the Chicago World's Fair. When the public saw the beautifully and safely lit buildings, they realized that Edison was wrong. Even Edison's own company eventually converted to using AC power, and it is the standard for electricity in the United States today.

THE WORLD'S HEAVIEST PIANO

Edison was a brilliant inventor, but sometimes he had some insane ideas. One was his idea for a concrete piano. Edison became infatuated with concrete and thought that it was the perfect building material. He filed patents for a concrete house, concrete furniture, and a concrete piano. Although he was right in thinking that the concrete would be very durable, he didn't consider how heavy concrete would be. The concrete pianos that were built were impossible to move, and they sounded weird. Concrete is good at muffling sound, and the pianos did not project music like a normal wood piano. But the concrete piano would not burn up in a fire!

THE WORLD'S HEAVIEST PIANO

~continued from page 98~

There were 11 concrete houses built, but they were so ugly that no one wanted to buy them. Concrete homes were a total flop. The one idea that did have merit was concrete furniture, but it took nearly 100 years to catch on. Furniture designers are now using concrete to pour freeform chairs and benches. Nobody is building concrete pianos.

A HEART FOR SCIENCE

Werner Forssmann was just an intern when he came up with the idea of cardiac catheterization. He was sure that he could administer drugs directly to the heart by threading a small tube through the veins of the arm and into the heart. His supervisors at the German hospital said he was crazy. It would be insanity to try such an experiment on a human. Too dangerous. Not worth the risk.

But Forssmann was sure he was right. And he was stubborn. He was determined to prove to his supervisors that he was correct. He studied several ways

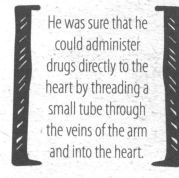

He was sure that he could administer drugs directly to the heart by threading a small tube through the veins of the arm and into the heart.

to insert the tube and decided that threading it through the jugular vein was too risky. He decided that a safer start point would be the arm. If he was successful, it could provide new ways of giving medicine and clearing blockage.

He asked for permission to try the experiment, offering his own body as the test subject. His supervisors refused. It was much too risky. Forssmann discussed his theories with operating room nurse Gerda Ditzen. He had to get her permission to enter the operating room and use the equipment. After he explained his scientific theories, Ditzen agreed to help with his experiment. She even volunteered

Insertion
Point

to allow Forssmann to run the tube through her veins to her heart. They both knew the experiment would technically be illegal because it had not been approved by any of the hospital supervising staff.

The two experimenters agreed to meet in the operating room and do the test in secret. It was early summer of 1929 when they met. Forssmann told Ditzen to lie on the operating table. He strapped her arms and legs down and pretended to get ready to inject her with the anesthetic. But in reality, he injected his own arm with anesthesia. When his arm was numb, Forssmann threaded the catheter tube through his own vein and toward his heart.

Then he released Ditzen and told her to call the X-ray room. Ditzen was angry at Forssmann for tricking her, but she rushed him down one floor to the X-ray room where he used a fluoroscope to help guide the catheter to the tip of his ventricular cavity. They documented the successful experiment with X-rays and showed them to the chief surgeon. Angry at Forssmann for pulling such a dangerous stunt, the chief surgeon reluctantly admitted that Forssmann's experiment was a success. Forssmann was allowed to continue his residency and published a paper about his discovery.

When World War II started, Forssmann was called upon to serve as a military surgeon for the German Army. He was eventually captured by the Allies and spent time in a prisoner of war camp. When the war ended, Forssmann was relieved to find that his wife had survived. He set up practice as an urologist and worked hard to earn enough money to take care of his wife and children. He had given up his ideas of cardiac catheterization.

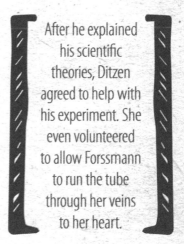

After he explained his scientific theories, Ditzen agreed to help with his experiment. She even volunteered to allow Forssmann to run the tube through her veins to her heart.

But in 1951, he was invited to visit a cardiac catheter lab that was opening in London. He was amazed to see his research put into action on real

Angry at Forssmann for pulling such a dangerous stunt, the chief surgeon reluctantly admitted that Forssmann's experiment was a success.

heart patients. In 1956, he received an even bigger surprise when he was notified that he was one of the winners of the Nobel Prize in medicine for the daring experiment he had conducted in 1929.

It took almost 30 years for Forssmann's experiment to be recognized for the groundbreaking work that it was. Today cardiac catheterization is a procedure that is done around the world to help diagnose and treat heart disease. And it all started with a stubborn doctor willing to operate on himself.

DR. DOGGENSTEIN

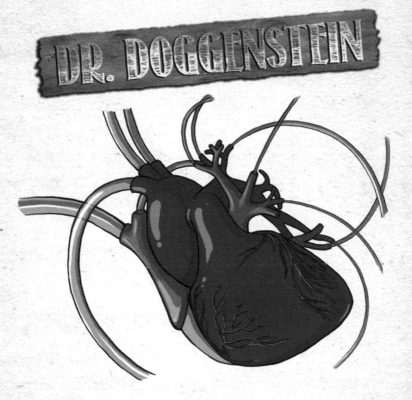

What is the one organ in the body that can never hold still? The heart. If the heart stops beating, then freshly oxygenated blood stops flowing to all the organs of the body, and the animal dies.

This had been a problem for doctors from the beginning of surgical history. If there was a problem with the heart, it was next to impossible to repair. They couldn't cut and stitch on a moving heart.

> They couldn't stop the heart from beating, or the patient would die. Heart disease was almost always a death sentence.

It was too dangerous. They couldn't stop the heart from beating, or the patient would die. Heart disease was almost always a death sentence.

But in the 1920s, a Russian scientist named Sergei Brukhonenko began some daring experiments to see if he could bypass the heart and keep blood flowing to the rest of the body. In other words, he wanted to let the heart stand still.

He called his invention the autojektor, and it worked with a series of tubes and pumps that pumped oxygen into the blood and pushed it through the patient's body. He proved its effectiveness by practicing on animals, most frequently dogs. He removed the heart of a dog and kept it beating while pumping blood through the body. Then he put the heart back in the dog and revived it. He tried this experiment over and over again until he was sure his autojektor worked.

Thrilled with his new invention, Brukhonenko wondered just what were the limits of the autojektor? Could he keep an animal alive without any heart and just the autojektor? Could he drain an animal of blood and use the autojektor to pump it back in and revive the animal? Could the autojektor keep a head and brain alive if the body was too badly damaged? That's when Sergei's experiments started to get very strange.

During the 1920s, many scientists used animals for their experiments. They believed that in order to advance science, it was sometimes necessary to sacrifice the lives of animals as test subjects. Brukhonenko went farther than most scientists. He learned that he could keep the severed head of a dog alive with the autojektor for several minutes. He was successful in draining blood from the body and bringing the dog "back to life." Unfortunately, the dogs were usually brain damaged from lack of oxygen and did not live very long.

By today's standards, the experiments that Sergei did seem to be very harsh and cruel—the work of a Dr. Doggenstein. But the work he did paved the way for modern heart surgery. His auto-jektor was the basis for the development of modern heart-lung transplant equipment.

Today, doctors at UCLA are developing a machine that keeps a heart beating when it is removed from the human body to be used in transplants. Currently donor hearts are injected with potassium chloride to stop the beating, and then the heart is packed on ice. It has to be placed in the waiting patient within 4–6 hours.

The new machine would allow hearts to be preserved in a more natural state and could allow for a longer time between removal and transplant surgery. This would allow the hearts to travel greater distances and improve the chances that somebody who needs a heart can receive one.

HEART IN A BOX

You can see the amazing new invention of Heart in a Box at https://www.youtube.com/watch?v=Fwd32Xa3uwc

HUMAN CRASH TEST DUMMY

Lawrence Patrick strapped himself into the seat and waited for the heavy metal pendulum to crash into his chest. Would it break his ribs? Would it crush his lungs? Would he live through the test?

During the 1960s, Patrick and his team of young researchers acted as human crash test dummies. They took hits to the chest from a 22-pound pendulum. They had their faces smashed with "gravity impactors," and Patrick took 400 rides on a rapid deceleration sled that mimicked a car crashing head-on into a brick wall. It was all for the sake of improving automobile safety.

Seatbelts were not standard equipment in automobiles until the 1960s. People didn't understand that that little strap of cloth could save them from serious injury or death. Many people believed that safety came from a bigger, stronger car. But scientists were concerned because as cars got bigger and able to travel at faster speeds, there were more and more deaths from auto accidents.

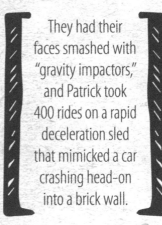

They had their faces smashed with "gravity impactors," and Patrick took 400 rides on a rapid deceleration sled that mimicked a car crashing head-on into a brick wall.

Researchers like Patrick needed to learn what effect a crash had on the human body and what would protect it. Crash test dummies had been invented during the 1950s, but they did not have sensor indicators. Inventors needed data that they could only get from human bodies.

They first tried doing experiments with live pigs because the internal anatomy of a hog is similar to that of a human. But the external anatomy of a pig is just too different, so they had to get information from human beings. When the testing was going to be too dangerous for living humans, they used cadavers. Patrick and his team learned how much pressure it took to crack a human skull by dropping a human cadaver down an elevator shaft.

Although it sounds gruesome, these tests were incredibly important. They taught scientists just how much the human body could withstand and set standards for vehicle safety. They also helped in developing dummies with readable sensors so that future humans would not have to serve as live crash test dummies.

Amazingly, Patrick survived all of the tests and lived to be 85 years old. He was awarded the A.W. Siegel Award for outstanding interna-tional research and contributions to crash injury protection. Every person who clicks on a seat belt has Lawrence Patrick to thank for mak-ing us a whole lot safer.

WHO'S DRIVING THAT CAR?

Inventors are still looking for ways to improve car safety, and their newest invention is the driverless car. The car uses GPS and computers to guide the car. Eventually, scientists plan for the cars to be able to talk to each other so there will be no need for traffic signals. Many people today are afraid that the computers might make a mistake or get hacked and cause an accident. But scientists point out that most airplanes fly on auto-pilot, and it has made air travel much safer.

ROCKET MAN

Flying an airplane in World War I was extremely dangerous. The newly invented planes were made of flimsy wood, cloth, and wires. They could be shot down by machine guns or crash in a ball of fire. Then something strange began happening to the pilots. As they flew higher and dove faster during combat fights, the pilots began passing out—*while they were flying the planes.*

Doctors were baffled and began calling the strange phenomenon "fainting in the air." In reality, the pilots were passing out because of the effects of gravity forces on the body.

Gravity forces, or G's, are the amount of pull on the body. One G is equal to what a person feels when he or she is sitting in a chair on Earth. When speeding up or slowing down very quickly, we feel more G's, like on a roller coaster. At the bottom of a hill on a roller coaster, you feel more G's and at the top of the hill the body feels less G's. Airplanes experience increased G's as they are moving fast and as they are turned to the left, right, or sent upward.

G forces also came into play when an airplane crashed. At the beginning of World War II, scientists believed that the human body could only survive 18 G's, or 18 times the force of gravity, in a crash landing. Because of this, cockpits were only designed to withstand 18 G's, but as the war went on, many pilots walked away from crashes that had much higher G forces. Doctors and scientists were amazed.

Dr. John Stapp was a physician in the Air Force, and he believed that what killed most pilots was not the G forces but the metal of the plane mangling the pilot's body. He decided to begin testing to see how much the human body could withstand. Could a pilot be saved if he ejected out of the plane instead of going down with it? What kind of parachute or protection could save the pilot?

As they flew higher and dove faster during combat fights, the pilots began passing out— *while they were flying the planes.*

No human had ever tested what gravity forces the body could survive. There was no data to help engineers build safer cockpits or design better parachute harnesses. Stapp decided that he would investigate the effect of G forces on the human body, and he would volunteer his own body as a test subject.

Stapp and his research team built a rocket sled in the American Southwest desert. The sled ran on rails and had an actual pilot's seat for the rider. A rocket was attached to the sled to push the seat forward as fast as possible. Then brakes, and later water, were used to stop the sled as quickly as possible. The fast acceleration and immediate deceleration created gravity forces on the human body.

The team spent a year testing and preparing the run before they launched a human. In 1948, they began testing the sled with human subjects. Stapp was the first and most frequent volunteer. He didn't like to allow any other volunteers to ride the rocket sled for two reasons: (1) because he feared for their safety, and (2) because he liked to know the test results personally. He felt he could make adjustments better if he had firsthand knowledge.

Stapp spent 5 years experimenting with the rocket sled. He strapped on more powerful rockets. He went from two rockets up to nine. His rocket sled could produce 50,000 pounds of thrust. And Stapp learned what the human body could endure.

When his body was hit with 18 G's, he experienced concussions, lost the fillings out of his teeth, and twice broke his wrist. But the worst problem

was with his eyes. The heavy forces caused the capillaries in his eyes to burst and gave him white-outs, where he had blurry vision and could not see. And this was when he was riding backward in the pilot seat. Facing forward, it was worse. Then, the blood was pushed up against his retinas and he experienced red-outs.

He strapped on more powerful rockets. He went from two rockets up to nine. His rocket sled could produce 50,000 pounds of thrust. And Stapp learned what the human body could endure.

Stapp proved that the eyes were the most vulnerable part of the body when facing high gravitational pull. Stapp also helped design better harnesses for parachutes and restraining straps for cockpits. He discovered that having pilots breathe pure oxygen for 30 minutes before flying would prevent the bends (getting sick from changes in altitude).

His final run was his fastest. In December of 1954, he launched with nine rockets for thrust and was clocked at 632 miles per hour. In 5 seconds, he slammed into two tons of wind pressure and then came to a stop. The gravitational forces made his

[The heavy forces caused the capillaries in his eyes to burst and gave him white-outs, where he had blurry vision and could not see.]

168-pound body act as if it weighed 7,700 pounds. He had survived more than 40 G's of deceleration and had become the fastest man on Earth.

When his sled came to a stop, he had to be immediately rushed to the hospital. All of the blood vessels in his eyes had burst. He had cracked ribs, broken wrists, and difficulty breathing. But Stapp recovered and had no lasting damage.

His experiment proved that a pilot could survive ejecting from an aircraft traveling at 1,800 miles per hour at 35,000 feet. He also proved that with an adequate restraining system, a pilot could survive a crash of 45 G's. Because of this, jet pilot seats were modified for stronger impacts.

Dr. John Paul Stapp continued working for better, safer airplanes and transportation for the rest of his career. He died in 1999 at the age of 89. When he died, he still held the record for the fastest human on Earth.

DEATH BY INVENTION

Inventors are often willing to do anything to create or improve an invention—they're even willing to *die* for the sake of science. These seven unlucky inventors were actually killed while they were working on their creations.

FRANZ REICHELT

DEATH BY PARACHUTE

Diving off the Eiffel Tower is never a good idea, even if you have invented a wearable parachute. Franz Reichelt was a tailor who lived in France in 1912. He was fascinated with the new invention of the airplane and was sure his invention of a wearable parachute would save the lives of pilots if their planes were damaged.

He tested his invention by dressing dummies in the parachute suit and throwing them off the Eiffel Tower. The dummies all survived the fall more or less intact. So Reichelt decided to climb up 187 feet and launch himself off the Eiffel Tower. The parachute failed, and Reichelt was killed the instant he hit the ground. The parachute suit was never put into production.

HORACE HUNLEY
DEATH BY SUBMARINE

Horace Hunley was a man ahead of his time. During the Civil War, he invented a hand-powered submarine that actually worked. He had visions of his Confederate submarine sneaking up on the Union ships and sinking them. The Union sailors would never imagine the Confederates had built an underwater fighting vessel.

The Confederate Navy was desperate to sink Union ships and began test runs with the submarine. During one test run in August 1863, the submarine got swamped and sank, killing all five crew members.

Hunley and the Confederacy were not willing to give up. They raised the submarine and began new test runs. In October 1863, Hunley went out with the crew and disaster struck again. Horace Hunley and seven other sailors were killed when the submarine went down.

Even after the inventor's death, the Confederate military was willing to try the submarine again. They raised the submarine, cleaned it up, and in February 1864, they launched the submarine again. This time it successfully attacked and sank the Union ship *Housatonic*. But the submarine never made it back to shore. All eight of the crew died. In all, there were 21 men killed experimenting with the Hunley submarine. The idea of underwater fighting was not truly successful until the Germans used the U-boat in World War I.

WILLIAM BULLOCK
DEATH BY PRINTING PRESS

William Bullock was an inventor during the Industrial Revolution and invented several tools that modernized farming, such as a hay press, seed planter, and grain drill. In 1843, he turned his attention to improving the printing press and invented a web rotary press that allowed for large rolls of paper to continuously feed through the press. This was much faster than hand-feeding individual pages into the press. This revolutionized the speed of printing, increasing the speed to a dizzying 30,000 sheets an hour.

But in 1867, Bullock had a terrible accident while he was making adjustments to one of his presses. His leg was crushed when it got caught in the machine. A few days later, his leg developed gangrene and had to be amputated. Bullock did not survive the operation. He died from the printing press injury on April 12, 1867.

OTTO LILIENTHAL

DEATH BY GLIDER

Otto Lilienthal was known as the glider king. As one of the pioneers of aviation, he invented a glider similar to hang gliders that are used today. From 1891 to 1896, Lilienthal made more than 2,000 successful glider flights. But his luck ran out on August 9, 1896: After making a few successful flights that day, his last flight ended in disaster. His glider pitched forward in the wind and plummeted to the Earth. Lilienthal's mechanic rushed him to the hospital, but there was nothing that could be done. Lilienthal's last words to his brother were "Sacrifices must be made." The inventor realized that he was risking his life for the advancement of science and was willing to die in the effort.

ALEXANDER BOGDANOV

DEATH IN SEARCH OF ETERNAL YOUTH

Many people have tried to invent a formula for eternal youth. Nobody has ever succeeded, but that fact didn't stop Alexander Bogdanov from trying. He decided that blood was the key to youth and in 1924, began experimenting with blood transfusions. He began giving himself blood transfusions and claimed that after several transfusions, his eyesight was improved and his balding had stopped. But in 1928, he took the blood of a young man suffering from malaria and tuberculosis. Bogdanov did not understand that disease could be transmitted through blood, and science had not yet learned about different blood types. Instead of eternal youth, Bogdanov died at the age of 55 from his own experiment.

VALERIAN ABAKOVSKY
DEATH IN PURSUIT OF SPEED

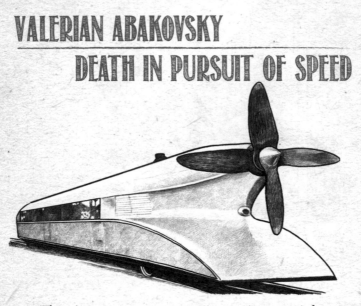

The Aerowagon was an invention straight out of science fiction. In 1921, young Russian engineer Valerian Abakovsky took a train engine and fitted it with an airplane engine and a propeller. His dream machine could travel at the amazing speed of 140 miles per hour. In 1920, the fastest cars in the world reached top speeds of 99 mph.

The Aerowagon was designed to shuttle Russian officials to and from Moscow, and in July 1921,

Abakovsky loaded up a bunch of Russian government officers and took them on a ride from Moscow to Tula. They arrived in Tula in record time, but on the way home, the Aerowagon flew off its rails and crashed. Abakovsky and five of the government officials were killed. The Aerowagon never ran again.

MAX VALIER
DEATH IN PURSUIT OF SPACE

In 1924, the idea of space travel seemed crazy to most people. But Max Valier was not most people. He was a trained machinist who had studied physics, and he had written articles on space travel, including "A Daring Trip to Mars."

He teamed up with Fritz von Opel and began experimenting with rocket-powered cars and aircrafts. He also founded the German spaceflight society, Verein für Raumschiffahrt. His rocket-powered cars moved at speeds higher than 100 mph and stunned fans throughout Germany. His inventions paved the way for solid rocket fuel engines and modern spaceflight. But in 1930, Valier was experimenting with an alcohol-fueled rocket when it exploded on his test bench. A piece of shrapnel severed his pulmonary artery, and he died within minutes. He was one of the first inventers to die for space experimentation.

INSANELY FUN

On hot summer days, there are two things kids are thankful for—Popsicles and Super Soakers. One was invented by an 11-year-old boy, and the other was created by a rocket scientist. Both of these insanely fun inventions were discovered by accident.

One cold evening in 1905, 11-year-old Frank Epperson was playing with a glass of flavored soda water and a stick. When he was called inside, Frank forgot about his drink and left it outside overnight. The next morning, he found he had created a frozen treat on a stick.

As an adult, Frank decided to sell his frozen dessert to beachgoers and vacationers. By 1924, he had a good business selling fruit-flavored ice on birch wood sticks. He applied for a patent and the Popsicle was born.

The Super Soaker was the accidental discovery of Lonnie G. Johnson, a successful NASA engineer and inventor. Johnson started inventing when he was a little boy growing up in Mobile, AL. He built a go-kart out of junkyard scraps and a lawnmower engine. He had a great time racing it along the highway until the police pulled him over. In 1968, Johnson entered his compressed power robot in the Junior Engineering Technical Society. Johnson won first prize and went on to study at Tuskegee University on an academic scholarship. He graduated with a B.S. in mechanical engineering and a master's degree in nuclear engineering.

Johnson went on to join the U.S. Air Force and help develop the stealth bomber. Then he went to work at NASA and helped engineer the Galileo mission to Jupiter and the Cassini mission to Saturn.

In his spare time, Johnson still liked to work on his own inventions. He was working on a model of an environmentally friendly heat pump one evening in 1982 and decided to test it in his bathroom. When he aimed the nozzle and pulled the lever, he sent a powerful blast of water into the tub. Johnson loved it. This was fun!

He now had two inventions to work on. He kept tinkering with his heat pump, but he also decided to perfect his "Power Drencher" and make it into an awesome squirt gun. It took 7 years of experimenting and selling the concept, but in 1989, the Super Soaker was born. It is still one of the top-selling toys in the world.

Johnson has used the profits from his Super Soaker to fund his research of the Johnson Thermoelectric Energy Converter (JTEC). If it works, the JTEC will be an advanced heat engine that can convert solar energy into electricity with twice the efficiency of existing models. It might not sound as fun as a Super Soaker or a Popsicle, but it would be an insanely important invention that could push the green technology revolution into the future.

Inventor's Lab

MAKE A BOTTLE SQUIRT GUN

ant to make a powerful squirt gun that your friends will never suspect? It's simple. You just need some air pressure.

MATERIALS

» Water bottle with lid
» Water
» Tack or large needle
» Bicycle pump with needle

First, use the tack or needle to poke a hole in the center of the water bottle cap. Then fill the bottle with water. Screw the cap tightly onto the water bottle.

Next, insert the needle of the bicycle pump into the hole in the lid and pump air into the bottle. This will add pressure to the bottle and make it squirt farther. Stop pumping when you feel the bottle is full.

Now you have a squirt gun that looks like a regular water bottle. You just have to press your thumb on the bottle, and it will squirt your friends and family.

Inventor's Lab

BUILD A MOVING FORCE MACHINE

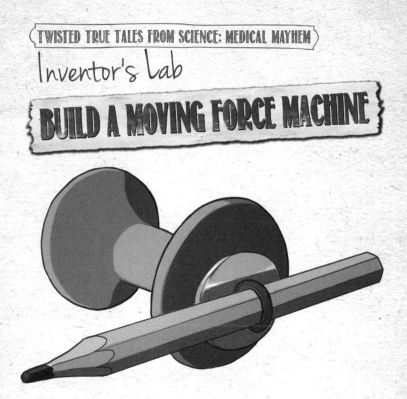

ou can experiment with the forces of gravity by making a moving machine.

MATERIALS

- » Empty spool for thread
- » Rubber band
- » Metal washer
- » Pencil
- » Tape
- » Toothpick

Slip the rubber band through the center of the spool. Place the toothpick through one loop of the rubber band and tape it down. Break off the ends of the toothpick so it doesn't extend beyond the edges of the spool.

On the other end of the rubber band, slip on the washer and then put the pencil through the rubber band loop. Wind up the pencil until the rubber band is tight. Then put the spool on the table, and watch your motion machine go.

BIBLIOGRAPHY

BOOKS

Carlson, B. W. (2015). *Tesla: Inventor of the electrical age.* Princeton, NJ: Princeton University Press.

Gribbin, J., & Gribbin, M. (1997). *Newton in 90 minutes.* London, England: Trafalgar Square Publishing.

Harrison, I. (2004). *The book of inventions*. Washington, DC: National Geographic.

Jack, A. (2015). *They laughed at Galileo: How the great inventors proved their critics wrong*. New York, NY: Skyhorse Publishing.

Jardine, L. (2004). *The curious life of Robert Hooke: The man who measured London*. New York, NY: Harper Collins.

Pickover, C. A. (1999). *Strange brains and genius: The secret lives of eccentric scientists and madmen*. New York, NY: Plenum Trade.

Robinson, A. (2006). *The last man who knew everything: Thomas Young, the anonymous polymath who proved Newton wrong, explained how we see, cured the sick, and deciphered the Rosetta Stone*. New York, NY: Pi Press.

Tesla, N. (2015). *My inventions: The autobiography of Nikola Tesla*. New York, NY: SoHo Books. (Original work published 1919)

Wearing, J. (2009). *Edison's concrete piano: Flying tanks, six-nippled sheep, walk-on water shoes, and 12 other flops from great inventors*. Toronto, Ontario: ECW Press.

WEBSITES AND ARTICLES

Alvarez, E. (2015). Lonnie Johnson, the rocket scientist and Super Soaker inventor. *Engadget.* Retrieved from https://www.engadget.com/2015/02/27/lonnie-johnson-the-rocket-scientist-and-super-soaker-inventor

American Institute of Physics. (n.d.). *Marie Curie and the science of radioactivity: War duty (1914-1919):* Radiology at the front. Retrieved from https://www.aip.org/history/exhibits/curie/war1.htm

American Medical Association. (1964). Stubbins H. Ffirth (1784–1820). *JAMA, 189,* 319–320. Retrieved from http://jama.jamanetwork.com/article.aspx?articleid=1163961

BBC. (n.d.). *Isaac Newton: The man who discovered gravity.* Retrieved from http://www.bbc.co.uk/timelines/zwwgcdm

Bernard, A. (2014). A cultural history of the elevator. *Pop Matters.* Retrieved from http://www.popmatters.com/feature/178128-lifted-a-cultural-history-of-the-elevator

Biography.com. (n.d.). *Lonnie G. Johnson.* Retrieved from http://www.biography.com/people/lonnie-g-johnson-17112946#early-life-and-education

Brown, A. S. (2010). The science that made Frankenstein. *Inside Science.* Retrieved from https://www.insidescience.org/content/science-made-frankenstein/1116

Brown, M. (1997). X-ray photographer: Elizabeth Fleischmann. *FoundSF.* Retrieved from http://foundsf.org/index.php?title=X-ray_Photographer:_Elizabeth_Fleischmann

Capanna, E. (1999). Lorenzo Spallanzani: At the roots of modern biology. *Journal of Experimental Zoology, 285,* 178–196. Retrieved from http://www.csub.edu/~ddodenhoff/biologyreport/rootsofmodernbiology.pdf

Cianciosi, S. (2007). *Sergei's litter.* Retrieved from http://www.damninteresting.com/sergei%E2%80%99s-litter

Connor, S. (2010). The core of truth behind Sir Isaac Newton's apple. *Independent.* Retrieved from http://www.independent.co.uk/news/science/the-core-of-truth-behind-sir-isaac-newtons-apple-1870915.html

Conradt, S. (2010). 10 things you didn't know about Isaac Newton. *Mental Floss.* Retrieved from http://mentalfloss.com/article/23631/10-things-you-didnt-know-about-isaac-newton

Cooper-White, M. (2013). Marie Curie mixed science and sex, and 9 other surprising facts about famous chemist. *Huffington Post.* Retrieved from http://www.huffingtonpost.com/2013/11/07/10-marie-curie-facts_n_4018373.html

Eggen, O. J. (2015). Tycho Brahe: Danish astronomer. *Encyclopaedia Brittanica.* Retrieved from http://www.britannica.com/biography/Tycho-Brahe-Danish-astronomer

The Elevator Museum. (n.d.). *Elisha Otis: Improvement in hoisting mechanism.* Retrieved from http://www.theelevatormuseum.org/otis.php

Encyclopedia of World Biography. (n.d.). *Henry Cavendish biography.* Retrieved from http://www.notablebiographies.com/Ca-Ch/Cavendish-Henry.html

Enersen, D. (n.d.). *Lorenzo Spallanzani.* Retrieved from http://www.whonamedit.com/doctor.cfm/2234.html

Heiss, H. W. (1992). Profiles in cardiology: Werner Forssmann: A German problem with the Nobel Prize. *Clinical Cardiology, 15,* 547–549. Retrieved from http://onlinelibrary.wiley.com/doi/10.1002/clc.4960150715/pdf

Jay, M. (2015). "O, excellent air bag": Humphry Davy and nitrous oxide. *MentalFloss.* Retrieved from http://mentalfloss.com/article/68148/o-excellent-air-bag-humphry-davy-and-nitrous-oxide

Jefferson Lab. (n.d.). *How do I make an electromagnet?* Retrieved from http://education.jlab.org/qa/electromagnet.html

Martin, W. (2013). *Giovanni Aldini's shocking experiments.* Retrieved from http://launchistory.blogspot.com/2013/02/giovanni-aldinis-shocking-experiments.html

Miklós, V. (2013). *13 unlucky inventors killed by their own inventions.* Retrieved from http://io9.gizmodo.com/13-unlucky-inventors-killed-by-their-own-inventions-509842353

Myers, G. (2014). Benjamin Franklin liked to take 'air baths'. *KnowledgeNuts.* Retrieved from http://knowledgenuts.com/2014/01/07/benjamin-franklin-liked-to-take-air-baths

National Museum of Health and Medicine. (2012). *U.S. Army Maj. Walter Reed: 1893–1902.* Retrieved from http://www.medicalmuseum.mil/index.cfm?p=about.directors.reed

O'Carroll, E. (2011). Marie Curie: Why her papers are still radioactive. *The Christian Science Monitor.*

Retrieved from http://www.csmonitor.com/ Technology/Horizons/2011/1107/Marie-Curie-Why-her-papers-are-still-radioactive

O'Connor, J. J., & Robertson, E. F. (2003). *Tycho Brahe.* Retrieved from http://www-groups.dcs. st-and.ac.uk/~history/Biographies/Brahe.html

Oxford University Museum of Natural History. (n.d.). *William Buckland.* Retrieved from http:// www.oum.ox.ac.uk/learning/pdfs/buckland.pdf

Palmquist, P. E. (1990). Elizabeth Fleischmann: A tribute. *Women Artists of the American West.* Retrieved from https://www.cla.purdue.edu/ waaw/palmquist/Photographers/Fleischmann Essay.htm

PBS. (n.d.). *Tesla: Life and legacy.* Retrieved from http://www.pbs.org/tesla/ll/index.html

PBS. (2006). The great fever: Yellow fever and the scientific method. *American Experience.* Retrieved from http://www.pbs.org/wgbh/amex/fever/peo pleevents/e_science.html

Rayovac. (2016). *The best way to make a homemade flashlight.* Retrieved from http://blog.rayovac. com/post/2016/09/26/make-homemade-flashlight

Roach, M. (1999). I was a human crash-test dummy. *Salon.* Retrieved from http://www.salon.com/ 1999/11/19/crash_test

Santa Maria, C. (2012). Mad science: Giovanni Aldini, corpse reanimator. *Huffington Post*. Retrieved from http://www.huffingtonpost.com/2012/05/15/mad-science-giovanni-aldini_n_1519723.html

Shakhashiri, B. Z. (n.d.). *Making things glow in the dark*. Retrieved from http://scifun.chem.wisc.edu/homeexpts/vaseline.htm

Sonnier, A. (2013). *Science for kids: Making a spool car*. Retrieved from http://www.learnplayimagine.com/2013/05/science-for-kids-making-spool-car.html

Spark, N. T. (n.d.). *46.2 Gs! The story of John Paul Stapp: The fastest man on Earth*. Retrieved from http://www.ejectionsite.com/stapp.htm

The Stapp Association. (2014). *Crash safety visionary*. Retrieved from http://www.stapp.org/stapp.shtml

Swain, F. (2013). Russians who raised the dead. *Slate*. Retrieved from http://www.salon.com/2013/06/14/russians_who_raised_the_dead

Today I Found Out. (2011). *The Popsicle was invented by an 11 year old*. Retrieved from http://www.todayifoundout.com/index.php/2011/08/the-popsicle-was-invented-by-an-11-year-old

Today in Science History. (n.d.). *Henry Cavendish*. Retrieved from https://todayinsci.com/C/Cav endish_Henry/CavendishHenry-Bio.htm

Tyson, P. (2007). All about G forces. *NOVA*. Retrieved from http://www.pbs.org/wgbh/nova/space/gra vity-forces.html

Vitelli, R. (2010). *Shy Henry*. Retrieved from http:// drvitelli.typepad.com/providentia/2010/10/ shy-henry.html

Vujovic, L. (1998). *Nikola Tesla: The genius who lit the world*. Retrieved from http://www.tesla society.com/biography.htm

Wayne State University. (2006). *Larry Patrick, pioneer auto safety researcher, 85*. Retrieved from https://wayne.edu/newsroom/release/2006/05/ 02/larry-patrick-pioneer-auto-safety-research er-85-2282

wikiHow. (n.d.). *How to make a water gun with a water bottle*. Retrieved from http://www.wiki how.com/Make-a-Water-Gun-with-a-Water-Bottle

Wikipedia. (n.d.). *Henry Cavendish*. Retrieved from https://en.wikipedia.org/wiki/Henry_Caven dish

Wikipedia. (n.d.). *List of inventors killed by their own inventions.* Retrieved from https://en.wikipedia.org/wiki/List_of_inventors_killed_by_their_own_inventions

Wikipedia. (n.d.). *Stubbins Ffirth.* Retrieved from https://en.wikipedia.org/wiki/Stubbins_Ffirth

Wikipedia. (n.d.). *Werner Forssmann.* Retrieved from https://en.wikipedia.org/wiki/Werner_Forssmann

Stephanie Bearce is a writer, teacher, and science nerd. She likes teaching kids how to blow up toothpaste and dissect worms. She also loves collecting rocks and keeps a huge collection of fossilized bones in her basement. When she is not exploding experiments in her kitchen or researching strange science facts in the library, Stephanie likes to explore catacombs and museums with her husband, Darrell.

MORE TWISTED TRUE TALES FROM SCIENCE

Twisted True Tales From Science: Disaster Discoveries
ISBN: 978-1-61821-574-1

London was once covered in a fog so polluted that it killed 12,000 people. The Aleppo earthquake killed 230,000 people, and a wall of water mysteriously wiped out the whole town of Burnam-on-the-Sea. All of these were catastrophic disasters, but they led to important discoveries in science. Learn about how the earth turned to liquid in New Zealand and what happens when a tsunami meets a nuclear reactor. These stories may sound twisted and strange, but they are all true tales from science!

MORE TWISTED TRUE TALES FROM SCIENCE

Twisted True Tales From Science: Explosive Experiments

ISBN: 978-1-61821-576-5

Two thousand years ago, Chinese scientists were looking for a medicine that would make them live forever. Instead, they blew up their lab and discovered gunpowder. Alfred Nobel blew up his laboratory twice before he discovered the formula for dynamite. Learn about the Apollo 13 and Challenger explosions and the strange space explosions caused by top secret Starfish Prime. These stories may sound twisted, but they're all true tales from science!

MORE TWISTED TRUE TALES FROM SCIENCE

Twisted True Tales From Science: Medical Mayhem

ISBN: 978-1-61821-572-7

Ground-up mummy bones, leeches sucking human blood, and a breakfast of dried mouse paste. It sounds like a horror movie, but those were actual medicines prescribed by early doctors. Medical students studied anatomy on bodies stolen from graves and had to operate on people while they were awake. Learn about the medicines that came from poison and doctors who experimented on themselves and their families. It's a twisted tale of medical mayhem, but it's all true!